The
Running Iron
Samaritans

NOV - 2003

***Also by Barry Cord
in Large Print:***

Cain Basin
The Deadly Amigos
Gallows Ghost
The Gun-Shy Kid
The Guns of Hammer
Hell in Paradise Valley
Last Chance at Devil's Canyon
The Long Wire
Six Bullets Left
Slade
Gun Junction
Two Graves for a Gunman

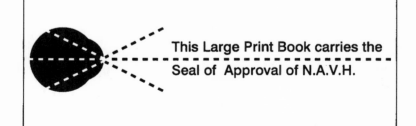

This Large Print Book carries the
Seal of Approval of N.A.V.H.

The
Running Iron
Samaritans

Barry Cord

Thorndike Press • Waterville, Maine

Published in 2003 by arrangement with Golden West Literary Agency.

Thorndike Press® Large Print Paperback.

The tree indicium is a trademark of Thorndike Press.

The text of this Large Print edition is unabridged.
Other aspects of the book may vary from the original edition.

Set in 16 pt. Plantin by Ramona A. Watson.

Printed in the United States on permanent paper.

Library of Congress Cataloging-in-Publication Data

Cord, Barry, 1913–
    The running iron samaritans / by Barry Cord.
        p. cm.
    ISBN 0-7862-5679-6 (lg. print : sc : alk. paper)
    1. Large type books.   I. Title.
PS3505.O6646R86 2003
    813'.54—dc21   2003055978

The
Running Iron
Samaritans

As the Founder/CEO of NAVH, the only national health agency solely devoted to those who, although not totally blind, have an eye disease which could lead to serious visual impairment, I am pleased to recognize Thorndike Press* as one of the leading publishers in the large print field.

Founded in 1954 in San Francisco to prepare large print textbooks for partially seeing children, NAVH became the pioneer and standard setting agency in the preparation of large type.

Today, those publishers who meet our standards carry the prestigious "Seal of Approval" indicating high quality large print. We are delighted that Thorndike Press is one of the publishers whose titles meet these standards. We are also pleased to recognize the significant contribution Thorndike Press is making in this important and growing field.

Lorraine H. Marchi, L.H.D.
Founder/CEO
NAVH

* Thorndike Press encompasses the following imprints: Thorndike, Wheeler, Walker and Large Print Press.

I

Long Jim Evers reined in his bronc, a scowl creasing his long face as he glared at his pint-sized companion.

"Forty miles from nowhere," he grumbled. "And me with my stummick riding my backbone! Dang it! Windy — ever since we left the Brazos to hunt up yore nephew in Goliath we ben heading into trouble!"

He waved a sinewy hand in wide sweep, embracing the inhospitable country ahead of them. "What's the idea cutting cross country from Las Cruces?"

"Shorter," his companion answered calmly. Windy Harris worked his chaw of tobacco into a pocket of his leathery cheek and spat over his roan's left ear. "An' cows. From what I heard back in Las Cruces, this section's full of mavericks an' sleepers jest waiting for a running iron. No law in forty miles —"

"And no grub in fifty!" Long Jim snapped. It was a consideration the long-shanked man viewed with a sense of imminent disaster.

Windy ignored this, to him, inconsequential remark. He was studying a small mound of stones ahead . . . a flat rock topped it and someone had drawn a crooked arrow with a piece of white chalk on it. Neither the rock mound nor the arrow had been recently constructed.

Long Jim followed his companion's gaze. "Injuns?"

Windy spat a stream of tobacco juice. "Mex."

Evers eyed him. "Howdja know?"

"Jest know, that's all."

Windy had a mysterious fund of knowledge, picked up through the years. To hear him tell it he had been left an orphan in the Michigan woods, worked as a water hauler for the lumberjacks, worked in mines, punched cows, filibustered in Central America, sailed around the Horn on a whaler, tracked Indians and fought the Johnny Rebs. All this before he had teamed up with Long Jim right after the Civil War.

Long Jim knew him as a liar, but not in things that mattered.

"We're close enough to the Mex Border to make it profitable," Long Jim muttered. Then, remembering he was hungry, he growled, "An' a hell of a long way from

8

anything resembling a restaurant —"

Windy cut him off. "That all you kin think of, yore stummick?"

"What else is there?" Long Jim snapped. He shifted in his saddle then, his tone growing serious. "Ain't no jobs left for us old folks, Windy. But I ain't ready to set in a rockin' chair an' wait for that grim reaper them sky pilots always talk about —"

"It's a young man's world," Windy agreed. "But I ain't sure they know what to do with it." He gazed off into the distance. "Once you get over forty nobody's hiring . . ."

"They got old folks' homes for us, I heard . . . there's a place up in Ohio —"

Windy's glance cut Long Jim off.

"You figgerin' to end up in one of them homes?" Windy asked sarcastically.

"At least they feed yuh," Long Jim snapped back. "I'm ready to eat the hide off a jack, if I spot one. In fact, right now I'm ready to —"

Out on the flats ahead, under a brush-topped butte, a light suddenly winked on. Long Jim's scrutiny made out the outlines of a rambling low building and the out-buildings of some kind of spread.

A hopeful smile lighted up his homely features. "Windy," he said, "We're saved. I see a ranch in yonder distance . . . I kin smell food already. Good, solid, home-cooked —"

Windy just grunted. "All right, Jim — let's go. 'Fore you starve us to death."

It was a surprisingly large spread, shaded by trees that were old. The main building was of yellow-painted adobe and thick timber framing and it was built around a huge patio in which was an enclosed well.

A high wall enclosed the ranchhouse and outbuildings, but it was breached in several places and it had never been repaired. It probably had been a grand place, once.

Giant pepper trees shaded the main house and several tall pecans towered above the corral, providing shade for a few horses from the fierce sun.

Now the evening shadows had softened most of the disrepair and the place seemed grateful for the night.

A man came out of the barn as they rode into the yard. He was a fast-stepping, horse-faced gent with a suspicious look in his eyes. Starlight, seeping though the trees, reflected from the rifle barrel he pointed at them.

"Howdy, gents," he greeted them. But his voice was neither warm nor friendly. "What's on yore minds?"

Windy Harris leaned on his saddle horn and stared innocently at the man. He was broad across the shoulders, thick through his Levi-clad waist, and he seemed less interested in finding out who they were than in getting them the hell out of here.

Windy said apologetically: "Just now it's that Henry yo're holding. A rifle muzzle sets uneasy on my stummick. . . . thanks," he chuckled easily as the man lowered the muzzle slightly. "Me an' this human beanpole are looking for the foreman of this ranch."

The blocky man did not move. His gaze narrowed on Long Jim's six-feet-three of saddled indolence, shifted to Windy's bare five-feet-four of wiry frame. An incongruous pair, these. Seamed of face and slouched in saddle — saddle bums, evidently. Then his attention was drawn to thonged-down Colts riding snug on lean thighs and a cold suspicion spread further across his face.

"You're looking right at him," he answered, curtly. "Spill your business and then ride out of here!"

Windy looked hurt. Long Jim edged his bronc up closer to the foreman and shook his head sadly. "Don't mind my partner, mister. We're harmless. We haven't had a decent meal since we left Las Cruces. We was riding up yonder, lost and helpless like, when we seen yore lights. So we figgered —"

Off to their right lamplight suddenly made a long oblong among the dappled shadows. A woman loomed up in the ranchhouse doorway. She was a tall, angular figure in faded clothing, her hair tied up in a bun on her neck.

"Rolly!" she called with quivering eagerness. "Who is it?"

The redheaded ramrod shrugged, eased his rifle into the crook of his right arm. "It ain't him, ma'am," he answered sullenly. "Just a coupla chuckliners askin' for a handout."

The woman came out to the broad, vine-covered veranda. The eagerness faded from her voice. There was a tired, hollow ring to it as she said, "Supper's ready, Rolly. Have them come in."

Rolly scowled. Windy and Long Jim were already out of saddle, heading for the stairs. He followed with soft, springy steps. Twice he paused to look out, beyond the yard, to the darkening prairie. Little lines etched his mouth corners. Then his attention swung back to the two old reprobates and his discontent deepened as he followed them into the house.

The meal was solid, the best Windy and Long Jim had eaten in a long time. Meat and potatoes and biscuits — and plenty of it. The lamp on the table made a circle of light that barely reached beyond them.

The angular woman picked at her food. She looked tired, without hope. Forty, perhaps, she looked twenty years older.

Rolly sat at one end of the long table, still scowling; he kept eyeing the wanderers with an intentness that caused Windy to squirm.

At the other end of the table sat a man in a wheelchair. Short, grizzled, he had a stubborn, harsh mouth and furrows in his ruddy cheeks. His name was Lincoln Fervans, and he owned the V Bar ranch. The woman was his wife, Lucy. They had no help save Rolly, who looked after things for them — and they made it known they weren't thinking of hiring.

This information had been given almost curtly by the crippled rancher. Windy and Long Jim were bidden to draw up chairs and dig in. Two extra plates were added to the three already on the table. They ate in silence, with none of the usually eager questions asked by people living in out of the way places.

Windy, stuffed long before his more voracious companion, felt the tension in the room. And he began to notice things now, little things that had escaped his first casual glance.

Rolly had deposited his rifle in a corner by the door, as though he expected to use it. The table had strange grooves in it — some old, several fresh, as though bullets had scoured its surface.

Windy kept his curiosity from showing in his eyes, but they narrowed slightly as he noticed ragged tears in the old cupboard across the room from the near window.

The uneasiness grew in Windy Harris. He could see Rolly eyeing the old wall clock, leaning forward intently, his fingers clenched on the table surface. Half past seven. Even as he looked the clock struck the half hour with a solemn, jangling stroke . . .

The lamp went then, its glass globe disintegrating. The sound of breaking glass mingled with the sharp crack of the rifle from the darkness of the yard.

Windy surged back, hearing Long Jim's surprised grunt. He lunged up in the sudden darkness, headed for the door. A squat figure cut across Windy's path. They collided and he heard the foreman's ugly voice swear in his ear. A hand shoved him roughly aside.

When Windy reached the porch more glass fell, as if something heavy had been thrown through the pane. Harris edged away from the swearing ramrod, the Colt in his fist held cocked and ready. His searching gaze caught a glimpse of a vague figure low-hung in the saddle of a black horse just clearing the adobe wall.

Windy's Colt slapped heavily, its report mingling with the sharper crack of Rolly's rifle. Adobe spurted a foot behind the fleeing rider. But the potshooter continued on, crossed a patch of starlight that revealed him as a small, indistinct figure wearing an anthill sombrero. Then he disappeared and the low drum of hoofs faded into the stillness of the night.

Windy remained by the door, staring off into the shadows. A long figure loomed up beside him. Long Jim's voice rasped in his ear.

"Get the potshooting galoot, Windy?"

Rolly eased toward them, still swearing in a flat monotone. He said: "Reckon that's all, gents — for tonight!" He said it as though the visit had been expected.

They reentered the house in silence and watched as Lucy Fervans lighted a candle and placed it on the table. She looked at them with a dull flatness in her voice: "You'll have to get more lamps, Rolly, next time you drive in to town. That was the last one we had."

Rolly shrugged, his eyes searching the dimly lighted floor. He paced forward, bent down to pick up something near the table leg. Windy's puzzled gaze followed him, then he turned to look at the crippled rancher still sitting in his wheelchair. There was a baffled rage in the man's eyes. His big-knuckled fists were tight about the chair wheels as though he had tried to lift himself up, force life into his paralyzed limbs.

Behind Windy Long Jim muttered: "Mebbe I'm loco, but —"

The foreman interrupted him. Rolly was holding a chunk of sandstone with a piece or paper wrapped around it. He undid the paper, glanced at it, then he handed it to the old cattleman.

"Just like the others," he said harshly. " 'Cept this time he's giving you a deadline. You got until Saturday to clear out!"

II

The crippled rancher slowly crumpled the message within his big fist. His wife walked to his side, placed a hand on his broad shoulder.

"We'll go, Lincoln. We've had nothing but misfortune since we bought this place. We can't hold out —"

She glanced at Rolly, as if for confirmation.

The foreman nodded. "He's got us by the throat, Mr. Fervans. And he knows this country better'n we do. We've tried everything. And you know how the sheriff feels —"

"He thinks we're crazy," the woman said bitterly. She turned toward the stove and the coffee pot. "Maybe we are — I don't know any more . . ."

Windy and Long Jim shifted uncomfortably, feeling out of place here and not knowing quite what to do. The others seemed to have forgotten their presence.

Fervans shifted in his wheelchair. "Did you see Strauss?" he asked his ramrod.

"Maybe if he gave us a hand —"

The foreman sneered. "I saw Box-Ear Strauss all right," he said harshly. "Strauss said he had enough trouble of his own watching out for the Diamond L without chasing after ghosts. He said something about losing cattle, too — and I didn't like the way he looked at me when he said it!" Rolly scowled. "The Diamond L may not be behind this Mex killer, but they sure as hell ain't losing any sleep over our troubles!"

Windy cleared his throat. "Sorry if we busted in at the wrong time, folks. Me and Jim didn't know. Who is this Miguel ghost?"

The old rancher chewed thoughtfully on his upper lip for a moment, eyeing them — then he held out the crinkled paper Rolly had handed him.

Long Jim looked down over Windy's shoulder. The message was simple: *This is your last warning. You have until Saturday. Miguel.*

Long Jim turned to the rancher. "One man — driving you off your spread?"

Lincoln's eyes glittered in futile anger.

"It ain't as easy as you think, stranger!" he snapped. "A man can't lick a thing he can't get close enough to fight!" He wheeled himself away from the table as Lucy put the coffee pot down on the table and started to clear away the mess made by the ambusher's bullets.

"I bought this spread over a year ago," Fervans went on. "There was a story went with it — that made me get it cheap. But I didn't hear the story until later.

"This place was once the old de Santoro hacienda — had been in Santoro's hands for generations. But the only rights they had to the place was the right of possession. Santoro claimed the land was granted to his ancestors years ago, by the King of Spain. But he never was able to produce the land grant. Or maybe he was too proud — he had given his word that he had the old document and he didn't feel he had to prove it to anyone.

"Anyway, about six years ago, the last of the Santoros were driven off this place by a man name of Elbow Johnson. Johnson showed up with a deed from the U.S. Government and backed it with guns. He had a craggy bunch of riders with him and when old de Santoro showed fight, he wiped him out. Some folks claim it was a massacre. A young son of Jose de Santoro, a seventeen year old named Miguel, got free. He went a little crazy, I reckon. He headed for the hills and then, for a coupla years, nothing was heard from him. Then he came back."

The rancher paused, his head bowed, his voice low. "It was hell — just plain hell. Johnson was no chicken-livered scoundrel — and he had *gunmen* riding for him. But this crazy Mex armed with a Sharps rifle he got somewhere, just broke them. He got Johnson long range, the second day — killed him while Johnson was standing right outside there, on the veranda. He wore Johnson's men ragged hunting him. He ambushed them 'till they were scared to go out alone. At night he near drove them crazy slamming lead into the place. They stuck it out for about four months. Then, what was left of that craggy outfit, quit cold. The hacienda went for a year without a buyer. Finally a Swede name of Carl Yost took over. He lasted six months . . ."

Fervans paused. His wife pushed a cup of coffee toward him, but the rancher seemed glad of a chance to tell the story again . . . he let the coffee lie.

"Eventually the sheriff took a hand. There ain't a better man, I'm told, than Sheriff Breller when it comes to cutting sign. And he was born in this part of the country. It took him four months to run

Miguel down. They shot it out on Standout Bluff. The sheriff swears he got two slugs into the young Mex before he fell into the river. But —"

Rolly interrupted, his voice hard. "The stories have it that Miguel's ghost is still riding over the range of his ancestors." His eyes held a sneering disbelief. "Mebbe so. But if the jasper that's been raising hell around here is a ghost, he's a blankety-blank solid one! And he sure knows how to handle a rifle!"

Fervans eased back into his chair. "We've been trying to hang on. I bought this spread legally. It's a good ranch, given half a chance. The day I took over, I had two good legs and I drove five hundred head of good beef stock on my range. Now Rolly tells me we're lucky if I can round up a hundred."

His voice turned bitter. "There was me, Rolly and my son working the spread. I had plans to hire a couple more. Now my son's gone and I'm a cripple. Got a slug in my back while riding the west line 'bout four months ago! Doc says I'll be in a wheelchair the rest of my life . . ."

Windy glanced at Long Jim.

Rolly said, "There's clean hay in the barn, strangers, case you care to hang

21

around until morning."

Windy and Long Jim grunted their thanks and followed Rolly outside. They left the old rancher staring at the shattered window.

As they crossed the gloomy yard Long Jim inquired carelessly: "What happened to the old man's boy, Rolly? This rifle-toting ghost get him, too?"

Rolly did not slow his stride. But his shoulders hunched forward in an apologetic gesture.

"It was the old man's fault, I reckon. Wally Fervans was one of them sensitive kids — the kind you got to handle easy. But Mr. Fervans is a hard man, and plumb set in his ways. He tried to break the boy to his way of thinking. Wally couldn't see it that way at all. The last argument they had the old man beat the hell out of his son. The kid was nineteen, then. He took his beating without a whimper. But I recall the way he looked at his father, after it was over — his face all bloody, his lips tight, his eyes gray pools of hell. He quit the spread that night, lit out for the Border. . . ."

Windy frowned. Long Jim muttered something about the folly of the young being surpassed only by that of the old.

Rolly left them in the barn, went back to

the ranchhouse. He had been bunking in Wally's room since the boy's leaving.

Something troubled Long Jim. He walked to the open door, squinted out at the dark rangeland. His gaze swung around to the dim light the candle made against the ranchhouse windows.

He said: "Hell!" and looked down at Windy, who was unconcernedly making a place for himself on a pile of clean hay. "I hope to hell this Mex ghost comes back tonight. Seems like we oughta do *something* for the grub we stowed away —"

"The grub *you* stowed away," Windy corrected. He settled back on the hay. "Hell, Jim, it ain't our affair. Come morning we'll head west and take a gander at the kind of mavericks the Diamond L have got running loose." He made a clucking sound in his throat. "Strauss, huh? Didn't we run acrost a mean hombre with a handle like that up in the Montanny country?"

Long Jim snorted, walked back toward the hay. "Sure, you idjit! He was a ghost, too. Don't you remember?"

Windy disdained reply. He squirmed a little, settled himself to sleep. But a train of thought persisted in crossing through his head.

"Ghost, too, huh?" He turned to Long Jim. "Say, maybe it ain't so far-fetched —"

But Long Jim was already snoring. Windy shrugged and settled back to sleep.

III

The morning sun was hot over the brown land, raising little shimmers of heat. Miles west of the V Bar, where a jumble of ravines and sandstone cliffs broke the expanse of rolling plain, a thin curl of gray smoke lifted against a tawny ravine wall and faded before it got above the sheer sides. A score of feet beyond the fire two broncs stood stiffly, forty feet of rope stretching taut from creased saddle horns. The sound of profanity faded slowly into the heated air.

"Lie still, drat yuh!" Windy Harris grunted. He dug a bony knee into the steer's heaving flank. Shifting, he attempted to dally a couple of turns around the animal's hind legs. The frightened steer lunged in a frantic effort to regain its feet, the ensuing struggle spilling the pint-sized rustler.

For a brief moment there was a flurry of legs, dust and chaps. Then it quieted, and Windy slowly untangled himself. He stood up, glaring at the hogtied animal, making queer gulping sounds in his throat. Finally his Adam's apple quit bobbing and an audible sigh of relief came from him.

The sound of unsuppressed laughter spun him around, a wrathful glare in his eyes. "What in hell *you* laughin' at, you overgrown, pinheaded mule?" he roared. "Can't a man swaller his chaw without you takin' a fit?"

Long Jim rocked weakly by the side of his hogtied animal. "Hell!" he gasped finally, tears in his eyes. "Damned if I ever saw anythin' like it! Like a sage hen, yuh was —"

He went off again.

Windy's glare changed. "Near two bits worth of ol' Harmony gone tuh hell!" he snapped. An uneasy expression filtered into his blue eyes.

Behind them the small fire crackled. The heat was boxed in between tawny slopes here; it was like a deep miasmic sea in which no wind stirred. Below them a creek slid through thickets with a soft, cooling murmur.

Long Jim straightened, getting control of himself. He looked down at his animal, his expression changing.

"We oughta be in Diamond L country here — an' these beeves cinch it. The brand on 'em is big enough to be seen from the ranchhouse." His eyes narrowed slightly and he peered closer at the animal's flank.

"Free iron branded, an' the hombre who done it was no artist. Huh," he grunted softly. "I'll be eatin' loco weed if the first iron on this critter wasn't a V Bar!"

Harris swung his attention to his trussed steer. "Looks like we ain't the only runnin' iron experts in this section," he commented. "Whoever worked on this one did a better job — but he was a mite careless closin' the diamond." He straightened, his leathery face scowling. "Mebbe this Box-Ear Strauss is makin' hay while Miguel's ghost rides, huh?"

Long Jim shrugged. He coiled his rope, walked to his range-wise roan and hung his reata from the horn. Swinging up into saddle he dropped his gaze to Windy.

"I got a hunch — an' it ain't good," he muttered. "I'm gonna take a look up the ravine —"

Windy nodded. What had seemed like the easy prospect of rebranding six or seven head and herding them through the broken country toward the Border was developing angles. Ghosts and brand-blotting and Box-Ear Strauss. . . .

He grunted, swung away from his

trussed animal for the iron in the branding fire. *Something,* he thought uneasily, *sure smelled on this range!*

The thud of sand-deadened hoofs jerked him away from the fire, his right hand flicking gunward.

He waited, his body alert, until view of the rider cutting around the sharp ravine eased him.

"Three Diamond L riders!" Long Jim snapped, pivoting his roan. "Headin' this way!" He cut across Windy's remonstrances concerning the trussed cows. "We ain't got time, yuh fool! Leave 'em! Let 'em guess!"

Windy whipped into saddle, crowded close to Long Jim. They swung back down the ravine the way they had entered it, crossed under a gnarled oak and suddenly pulled up. Ahead of them a shod hoof clanged sharply against stone!

Long Jim threw a glance back to their fire. His thin face tightened.

"Trapped! Looks like here's where two old fools come to the end of a rope!"

His shoulders hunched as his eyes swung over the tawny ravine walls. The stream here slid close to the abrupt barrier and Long Jim's questing gaze stopped at a slit in the wall beyond, like a wedge cut into the cliff.

28

"Mebbe we kin make it in there," he suggested.

He glanced at Windy as his partner didn't reply and was startled by his companion's pale face, the strange flicker in his eyes. He had never seen Windy like this before.

"First time I ever saw *you* get white around the gills, Windy. Scared?"

Windy straightened in saddle, snapped back weakly: "You'd get pale, too, yuh beanpole — if you had jist swallered yore chaw! Damn — it's shore raisin' hell —"

They splashed up the stream, crowded through screening bushes and entered the slit. It was a fault in the rock wall, about seventy feet deep, narrowing at every foot.

They dismounted and led their cayuses in 'till they could go no further, then they wrapped reins around a rock and left them, sliding back toward the opening with ready rifles.

They didn't have long to wait. A rider appeared, jogging a big-chested white horse. A slim, wiry youngster with a carbine tucked under his right leg, a black hat tipped rakishly over his right eye. He looked hard, bitter and dangerous.

His gaze froze on the tell-tale fire, the hogtied steers. The rifle slid into his hands with smooth, practiced motion. He scanned the canyon scene intently, then advanced cautiously toward the branding fire.

As the youngster passed them, Harris muttered: "Here's where we pull our stakes, Jim. This country's gettin' too cussed crowded for two pore rustlers like —"

Long Jim's fingers closed tight on his shoulder. "Wait! That kid — he looks a lot like that crippled rancher we et with last night. Mebbe —"

The kid was dismounting. He looked warily around, walked toward the steers. He paused by the almost dead fire, picked up Windy's running iron. He walked to one of the cows, squatted by it, studied the carelessly made Diamond L brand.

Three riders appeared around the bend. The youngster dropped the iron, started to run for his ground-reined cayuse.

A rifle barrel glinted in the hands of a gnome-like Diamond L rider. A spurt of flame showed, a sharp crack sounded. The Kid twisted in mid-stride, went down heavily. He clawed at the dust, pushed himself up to one knee. He finally lifted himself to his feet, his left arm limp, and faced the oncoming riders on unsteady legs.

The two oldsters who were the cause of

it watched through hard eyes. All thought of flight was gone from them. They were old hands at this game; they knew what would follow.

The Diamond L riders bunched up before the youngster, rifles glinting. They were as craggy looking hombres as Harris and Long Jim had ever lined up in their sights. The gent who had plugged the kid was squat, seemingly as wide as he was tall, and long-armed. He sat saddle of a horse that dwarfed him.

The other two were lean, raw-boned, stubby-profiled; they looked like brothers.

One of them took his coiled rope and eyed the youngster with loose-lipped smile. The gnome-like rider slipped out of saddle and walked to the trussed steers. He picked up the running iron, examined it, dropped it to the ground. He cut the cows loose, watched them lumber away into the brush.

Turning, he snapped orders. The man with the reata shoved the kid forward, jerking his thumb toward the gnarled oak.

Harris caressed the barrel of his rifle. He said softly: "They ain't losin' any time, Jim. They've got it all figgered out. An' the kid's the goat. What you aimin' to do about it?"

Long Jim frowned. "We got the boy into it. 'Sides, I don't like that midget, nor his friends." He grinned down at the mustached bantam as he eased his rifle into the crook of his long arm. "He's yore size, Windy — you take him."

The Diamond L men had the boy astride his big white horse, arms bound behind him, under the big oak. And they were working fast. The gnome whipped one end of the rope over an overhanging branch, started to widen the slip noose. He leered at something the boy said.

"We ain't got time for the law, Fervans. It's too far, anyway. We snapped you redhanded, usin' a runnin' iron on Diamond L beef. We've been losin' a lot of beef, ever since yore pop started that cock-an'-bull story about Miguel's ghost. This cinches it for me. Yore pop's been runnin' a bluff — hidin' his rustlin' under cover of that ghost yarn. Even the story about you an' him breakin' up was a fake. You wanted the Diamond L to think you was out of the country so you both could work yore little game —"

"That's a lie, Card!" the boy gritted. Pain beaded his forehead with sweat. "And you know it! Why don't you tell the truth? There's no one to hear you. You read the signs around the fire. There were two men doing the brand blotting. Reckon they heard you coming and hightailed it. Or maybe the whole thing was a Diamond L setup, and like a blundering fool I came riding into it. But I saw enough, Card. Those Diamond L branded steers were original V Bar!"

Card grinned as he toyed with the noose. "Mebbe you have seen enough at that. But I reckon you'll be doin' the rest of yore snoopin' in hell —"

He paused, stiffening with surprise as he caught sight of an incongruous pair shuffling toward them. The tall scarecrow had a rifle in the crook of his right arm, a Colt .45 thonged down on his right hip. The bantam beside him walked as if he creaked. His rifle was carried loose in his right hand, muzzle pointing toward the sand.

Long Jim said casually: "Yo're makin' a mistake, gents. Me an' my partner here, Windy, was the ones thinkin' of doin' a little runnin' iron work on them steers when you butted in." A cold grin cracked his long face. "That shore was a sloppy job you boys did on them V Bar critters. Reckon the brand blotters around here need lessons in their trade."

Card sneered, the grip of surprise easing

in him. This was better than he had hoped for. Like the boy had pointed out, he had read the signs — he had known it was not Fervans who had built that fire, roped those steers. Whoever it was must have noticed the careless branding. And he had not liked the thought of someone riding around with that information.

But now —

His small reddish eyes slanted to his two companions, narrowed meaningly. These two old fools would never live to talk to anyone! They had rifles in their hands; did they really believe that was enough to hold Card, Cheeky and Sturgeon?

He minced his cayuse to one side, thick lips twisting insolently. "So you two jaspers want to show the Diamond L how to blot brands?" He shook his head. "How you two old fools lived this long is beyond —"

His long right arm whipped up, spinning a Colt. He was still grinning, and he died like that. Windy's slug had passed clean through his heart.

Sturgeon, leveling his gun with desperate speed, stiffened as Long Jim's rifle cracked. He slid forward, hit the ground a moment after Card.

Cheeky had time to shoot twice, both wild. He was cursing as the two oldsters who used rifles like he had never seen them used before, fired again. Windy's slug got him in the left eye — Long Jim's over the heart as he started to sag in his saddle.

The sharp reports faded slowly down the ravine. The youngster held his frightened horse with his knees and stared with pained, wondering eyes at the three sprawled Diamond L gunmen.

Windy Harris was complaining: "There yuh go, Jim — wasting lead again! Two slugs for one polecat —"

Long Jim grunted angrily as he looked down to the clean sheared rip in his boot where Cheeky's first shot had passed.

"My best pair of boots!" he groused, disregarding the fact that they were his only pair. "Dang it, Windy — they cost me forty dollars in Cheyenne, an' yuh let that squint-eyed sidewinder —"

He cut himself short as he saw the youngster start to sway . . . he crossed quickly to the boy, cut him free and eased him out of saddle.

The boy winced as Long Jim ripped his shirt from his shoulder, exposing an ugly-looking gash.

Windy came up and gave the bullet wound a casual glance. "Not too bad," he commented, "for a danged fool who could have had his head shot off."

The boy pulled himself together and stared angrily at the oldster.

"Reckon we oughta take him back to the Fervans spread," Windy said to his partner. "They'll take care of him —"

The youngster jerked back, his eyes narrowing. "You ain't taking me anywhere, Grandpa!"

Windy eyed him with little tolerance. "Yo're that old rancher's son, ain't you? Walter Fervans?"

"Yeah," the boy admitted, "I'm Walter Fervans. But I ain't going to no ranch —"

Long Jim put in mildly: "Don't be a fool, boy. Yore paw an' maw are eating their hearts out for you. Besides, yore old man's hurt . . . got a bullet in his back some time ago that left him a cripple. He's in a wheelchair right now and he needs you —"

"My father doesn't need anybody," the kid snarled, "well or crippled! Least of all me!"

"Now that's a damn fool thing to say!" Windy snapped.

Walter gave him a disrespectful look. "Thanks for giving me a hand with those rustlers," he said, but his tone held little gratitude. "And I can take care of myself. Like you said, grandpa, it ain't too bad."

He turned to mount his horse.

Windy grabbed him by the slack of his pants, pulled him back.

"Yo're going back to yore paw, whether you like it or not!" he snapped.

Wally Fervans dropped his hand to his gun. He winced as Windy's muzzle prodded him none too gently in the pit of his stomach.

"Yo're more stubborn than yore old man," Windy snarled. "For two cents —"

"Make it three pesos, *señor*," the voice behind them interrupted. It was a crisp, feminine voice — and decidedly unfriendly.

Windy turned, shouldering Long Jim aside as he did so. The bullet nicked the top of his hat as it went by, the rifle report close, bouncing back from the hot hills.

He froze, his Colt still gripped in his right hand, eyeing with bleak anger the unwavering muzzle of a Winchester carbine held by the rider who had come up out of the ravine behind them.

She was small and Mexican and even in the shadow of a huge anthill sombrero Windy could see she was young. Much too young and too pretty, he reflected, to go around shooting at people she didn't know. She was wearing a caquero outfit, green velvet pants and jacket and a white silk shirt. The outfit looked like it could stand a cleaning.

"The gun, *señor* — *drop it!*"

Long Jim caught the instinctive tightening in Windy's face and he cut in quickly: "Hell, she's a girl, Windy . . ."

Windy sighed as he dropped his gun.

Wally Fervans grinned as he shoved Windy aside and hauled himself painfully into saddle.

The girl said crisply: "It is only because you are old and foolish that I do not shoot you." She glanced at Wally as he rode alongside. "Did they hurt you?"

He shook his head.

"Let's go, Maria." He was holding himself stiffly in saddle; only pride kept the pain from his voice.

Windy said disgustedly: "Yeah, go ahead. You make a fine pair."

Maria swung toward him with the rifle. Wally shoved the rifle muzzle aside. "They won't bother us," he said. "They probably saved my life."

Long Jim said: "What about yore paw?"

Wally Fervans' lips curled with an old bitterness. "My father threw me out a year ago. Far as I'm concerned, mister, he can go to hell!"

They backed their horses toward the ravine, then whirled, rode quickly out of sight. The sound of their passage lasted but a few moments, then the silence closed down around Windy and Long Jim.

Long Jim shook his head. "Ain't right . . . the way that boy feels about his pa."

Windy picked up his Colt, brushed sand from it, shoved it back into his holster.

"Hell with it," he grumbled. He eyed his partner with a belligerent stare. "Stick our noses in trouble and what do we get?"

Long Jim was staring off in the direction Maria and Wally had taken. "Reckon they're two of a kind, that old man, Fervans, and his boy — too damned stubborn to give an inch."

Windy shrugged, turned to his horse.

"Time we left," he growled. He glanced at the dead men. "Some of their friends could be riding down this way anytime."

But Long Jim wasn't paying attention to him.

"Notice anything familiar about that girl, Windy?"

Windy paused, eyeing his partner with suspicious stare. He knew from long experience what was behind Long Jim's seemingly casual question.

"No," he said sharply. "And I don't cotton to girls who take a shot at me."

"Too dark last night to make out anything for sure," Long Jim cut in, "but I swear it could be that girl who shot up the Fervans place."

"Miguel's ghost!" Windy's voice held a heavy sarcasm.

Long Jim shrugged. "Does seem strange, the boy and this Mexican girl shooting up his father's place." He knuckled his long jaw thoughtfully. "Seems a bit too much, even for a kid who hates his father."

Windy came up leading Long Jim's horse. "It ain't our trouble, Jim." He handed the reins to his partner. "Nothing worse than two old coots horning in where they ain't wanted."

Long Jim nodded slowly. "Yeah. Reckon yo're right." He mounted, looked off. "Still . . ."

"We've got troubles of our own," Windy cut in harshly. "You gonna hang around and let it catch up with us?"

Long Jim grinned. The logic of this was inescapable. He wheeled his horse around and followed Windy out of the canyon.

IV

Many men had pushed their way through the batwings of Mal Oysterling's BLACK ARROW BAR in the course of its short but vivid existence. But none such as the incongruous pair that came arguing into his place of business this drowsy summer afternoon.

Oysterling straightened irately; he had been dozing behind his bar and this unwelcome intrusion jarred on his sensitive nature. He was a shaggy giant, one-eyed and heavily bearded. The scowl that came into his face did not add to his appearance.

Neither Long Jim nor Windy noticed that scowl. They were in the midst of settling a grave problem and Long Jim finally hit upon the time-tested method of flipping a coin.

"Heads we eat, Windy — tails we drink?"

Windy Harris peered suspiciously up at his towering companion. A thin layer of trail dust caked his face. He licked dry lips, nodded watchfully.

"All right, you human beanpole. Tails we likker up." His eyes narrowed on the coin

41

his partner produced. "Wait a minnit!" he halted proceedings. "I want a look at that two bits."

Long Jim drew himself up with an injured air. "Hell, Windy, you don't think that I —"

"Naw," Windy grinned. "Jest my suspicious nature. That's better," he muttered as Long Jim slipped the bogus two-bit piece back into his vest pocket with a mournful gesture.

Oysterling's scowl deepened. He was accustomed to having strangers eye him with wary respect when they entered, for the ill fame of the BLACK ARROW BAR and its giant owner were well known to most who traveled the southern trails.

But these two oldsters acted as though they were alone, oblivious to their surroundings and the craggy gents craning soiled and leathery necks from tables along the cooler back wall.

Long Jim produced a silver dollar with reluctant gesture, spun it up under Oysterling's nose, slapped his palm over it when it hit the wet counter top.

Very cautiously, as though life itself hung in the balance, Long Jim lifted his hand.

Windy relaxed with a thirsty sigh. "Tails." He turned to the barman, disregarding the black scowl with an ingenuous grin and said: "Fill 'em up, boy. Me an' Long Jim are likkerin' up!"

Oysterling stared at the pint-sized man. *Boy!* He started to reach under the counter for his bung starter.

But Windy was turning away, watching Long Jim slide the silver dollar across the bar. Long Jim's expression was rueful, but the shorter man showed him no sympathy.

It was Windy's firm opinion, bolstered by years of constant companionship, that the more Long Jim ate the hungrier he got, until now he had reached a state wherein he was continually famished.

"Danged if yuh ain't got more stummicks than a camel," he observed cheerfully, grinning at his partner's discomfiture. "Hell, we jest et this morning. An' the meal yuh stowed away would have lasted any man a week!"

Long Jim disdained reply. He snagged the bottle Oysterling set up on the counter before Windy could get his hand on it and poured himself a drink with tantalizing slowness.

"I hope this varnish is fair," he muttered hollowly to the one-eyed bartender. "The stuff they served us at the last place wasn't fit to dip sheep in."

He turned to Windy. "Well, here's how . . ."

The afternoon wore on. The two oldsters drank steadily, evidently putting behind them the events of yesterday. Lincoln Fervans' troubles, and his son's, were really none of their business, they had concluded. And, from here, they had decided to head for the Mexican Border, hoping to pick up a few mavericks on the way.

Behind the bar Oysterling passed from scowling irritation to open-mouthed wonder and finally to sheer, blinking amazement. The interest of the shifty-eyed patrons of the BLACK ARROW passed from desultory stud and blackjack to the two cheerfully wrangling strangers who downed Oysterling's potent brew without apparent effect.

At drink number nine Oysterling sagged unbelievingly against his back shelves, his one good eye wide and distrusting. No one had ever taken nine straight shots of the rotgut he served and remained on his feet!

Windy's foot slipped off the brass rail and he steadied himself against the counter.

"Dang it, Jim," he complained, brushing a gnarled fist across his slightly blurred eyes, "must be something I et. I generally start with nine as a warmer-upper."

44

Long Jim turned with great deliberateness. He braced his long frame against the bar and surveyed the dingy saloon. The staring faces were slightly blurred; the batwings were staging a slow, rhythmic dance.

Long Jim shook his head. Turning, he leaned on his elbows and squinted at the open-mouthed bartender.

"Dig up another bottle of that redeye, boy," he said thickly. "Me an' Windy are celebrating."

Windy eyed him owlishly. "What *are* we celebrating?"

Long Jim frowned. "St. Patrick's Day. A li'l late," he conceded, "but —"

The clatter of hoofs, the jingle of spurs, announced the arrival of riders before the BLACK ARROW. Boots scuffed, made thumping noises on the wooden step. The batwings creaked, slammed violently against the scarred inner wall.

There was tawny hill-dust on the entering man's thick shoulders, veiling the nickel shine of his prominently displayed deputy's badge. A pair of flapping, oversized ears jutted from under a soiled black hat, overshadowing a bulbous nose that fists had hammered across a craggy face. His eyes were gray, cold as chilled steel.

Right now they were somewhat baffled; the men he had been looking for seemed to have vanished, leaving behind three of his best men sprawled and lifeless behind a dead branding fire.

He was wearing a grouch when he came stomping inside the saloon and the men close behind him walked warily, ready to jump at his first snapped order.

Oysterling closed his mouth, his scowl coming back to his villainous face. His good eye slanted to the now wobbly old-sters who, arms around each other, were lifting lusty if unharmonious voices in their partially remembered rendition of an old Irish song: *The Son Of A Gambolier*:

> *. . . I'm a rambling wretch of poverty, from*
> *Tip'ry town I came . . .*
> *I'm a rambling wretch of poverty, and the*
> *son of a gambolier . . . the son of, the*
> *son of, the son of a gambolier . . .*

Oysterling's scowl spread. This was no way for strangers to act when Box-Ear Strauss came to town . . . no way at all.

Box-Ear Strauss stopped an arm's length away from the bar. He was tired, thirsty and irritated and the two men barring his way were like a red flag waved in his face.

He dropped his hand down to one of the two guns strapped to his waist, and then, a sudden vague familiarity about them nagging at him, he said harshly: "Well, I'll be damned!"

His voice froze the men at the card tables and caused his followers to suddenly spread out, hands sliding down to slick gun handles.

Strauss took a step toward the unheeding, warbling oldsters.

"I'll be totally damned!"

The bellow forced itself past Long Jim's heroic attempt to feel sorry for the poverty-stricken wretch in the song. He turned to face Strauss.

The bar room was shifting amazingly and so were the two burly figures he saw standing in front of him.

He chuckled. "You probably will, fella . . . you probably will." Then, as his gaze steadied somewhat and his attention was drawn to the man's prominent ears, he stiffened.

He put a hand on his partner's arm, a warning tingling down his spine.

"Hold it, Windy —"

But the smaller man shrugged him off. "Mister," he said, grinning loosely, "yuh got the biggest ears alongside an elephant's.

Flap 'em — I want to see you fly . . ."

Strauss started to draw his gun. Long Jim swore softly as he came up with his long-barreled Colt; he jammed it with uncommon rudeness into Box-Ear's stomach.

The Diamond L foreman seemed to wrap himself around that blued barrel. Windy eyed Long Jim with owlish admiration. Then he stepped forward, took hold of one of Box-Ear's lobes and yanked. A gasp went up from the stunned audience. Windy put his palm into the foreman's face and shoved.

Strauss staggered backward, tripped and sat down heavily on the floor. His face was a lemon green and his eyes showed a lot of white.

Long Jim looked sad. The appearance of Box-Ear in town had cleared the fog from his brain, but his instincts were still dulled and he forgot the patch-eyed saloonkeeper at his back.

He said quickly to his partner, "We better get to hell out of here."

Oysterling cut him short by bringing the whiskey bottle down on Long Jim's head.

Liquor cascaded over Long Jim. He staggered away from the bar, his drawn Frontier jarring its loads aimlessly into the floor in front of him as men scattered wildly.

Box-Ear snarled. "Get them alive, boys! For the rope!"

Long Jim was swept back against his partner, whose fogged brain was just coming to the realization of what they faced. The flurry raged throughout the saloon. Chips, men and tables tangled.

Oysterling, coming around the bar to take a hand, ran into a solid, bony fist that tipped him back, sent him staggering dazedly among the wreckage of a table.

Finally the flurry subsided. A mass of men slowly untangled themselves from two recumbent and very battered figures.

One Diamond L rider, a slim, toothy gent fingered a swelling eye and spat out a tooth.

"Holy sufferin' hell!" he mumbled. "It ain't possible!" He looked down at the two unconscious oldsters. "Who would'a' thought it, lookin' at 'em? A buzz saw, that runt — an' the beanpole hits like a piledriver!"

He looked around at the others who displayed a various array of bruises. "Do they always fight like that — or is it only 'cause of Oysterling's rotgut?"

Strauss, still looking liverish, walked to the group standing around the recumbent figures. He kicked Long Jim twice in the ribs.

The rider next to him said through swollen lips: "Well, we got 'em for you, Strauss. But what are we gonna do with 'em? Jest a couple of drifters —"

"Drifters, hell!" the Diamond L foreman snapped, his strength returning. "These are the gents behind all the trouble in the territory . . . the same who've been rustling us clean. They're the hombres who killed Card, Cheeky an' Sturgeon, too!"

The rider looked dubious. "These two?"

"Sure," Strauss snapped. "They circled around and beat us into town, figgerin' we wouldn't know them and wouldn't be looking for them in Mesa City."

Long Jim was beginning to stir.

Strauss kicked him in the ribs again. "All right, boys — we know what to do with rustlers. Let's get them outside."

His men complied. They filed out of the saloon, burdened with the two dazed, barely conscious strangers.

Oysterling sagged against his bar and surveyed what was left of his saloon through his puffed eye.

"Two of them," he muttered. He couldn't believe it. "Two of them . . . old enough to be settin' in rockin' chairs. *And they were drunk!*"

V

Long Jim came fully conscious astride his bronc with his hands tied behind his back and a noose being slipped over his head. He glanced at Windy, who was in similar circumstances. Both were surrounded by villainous-looking hombres who seemed awfully anxious to pull on the rope.

The little man looked as though he had fallen in front of a stampeding herd. There was blood in his bristly mustache and it streaked his grizzled chin. One eye was completely closed.

Long Jim spat blood from a cut inside his cheek. His entire body ached and there was a sharp pain under his right ribs where Strauss' booted toe had landed. He could feel the throbbing of an egg-shaped lump on his head and the sharp odor of raw whiskey from his still damp shirt reminded him of how he had gotten that lump.

Box-Ear Strauss pushed his way through the men ringing the big oak tree in the town square. He barked: "Ready?" to the men holding the ropes.

Long Jim resigned himself to his fate. But Windy was the kind of man who'd go into hell still arguing.

He said, "Hey, wait a minnit, gents!" The bantam's one good eye swiveled toward Box-Ear. "This thing looks kinda hasty to me, Box-Ear. Mebbe Long Jim did stick his smokepole into yore stummick kinda rough-like. But Jim never had any manners, anyhow. Still, this is the first town we've seen where men get hung for such a playful offense —"

"You ain't hangin' because of what happened in the Black Arrow Bar," Strauss sneered. "You know damn well why! Yo're the rustlers who've been cleanin' out Diamond L an' V Bar stock. Probably the same gents who shot up old Lincoln Fervans, too!"

Long Jim shook his head in disbelief. He looked at Windy — his partner's mouth hung open at such brazen effrontery.

Mavericks and sleepers were their stock in trade. And brand-blotting they had raised to a fine art. But here in this country south of the Littlejohns they had come merely as travelers, peacefully bent, passing through.

Box-Ear roared: "Up with them, boys!

They've been seeing daylight long enough."

"*Wait!*"

The command sheared through that sun-blasted square brought a sudden halt to the proceedings.

The rangy, hard-eyed man who rode his big roan horse among that cluster of men wore a badge on his dusty blue shirt, a Colt Peacemaker on his thigh. His eyes were light gray, piercing. They turned on the Diamond L foreman with cold regard.

"What you up to, Strauss?"

Box-Ear eyed the lawman with sullen respect. "Hanging a coupla rustlers, sheriff. Caught 'em redhanded."

"Where's Slim?"

Box-Ear shrugged. "Hell, I don't know where yore deputy is. Sleeping somewhere, most likely."

"Where did you get that badge?"

The Diamond L foreman scowled. "Slim wasn't using it, so I —"

Sheriff Breller held out his hand. "Give it to me!"

Box-Ear unpinned the badge and tossed it to the sheriff. Breller swung his attention around to the two men with their necks in a noose.

"Cut them down!"

Box-Ear reacted angrily. "Sheriff — they

killed three of my men!"

"You see them do it?"

The Diamond L foreman hesitated, "No. But they —"

"Cut them loose!" the sheriff snapped. "We'll do this legal . . . not with a lynch mob. They'll stand trial. If they're found guilty, we'll hang them right here!"

A couple of men slipped the nooses from Windy and Long Jim and untied their hands. They were hauled down from their mounts and marched off to jail.

The Mesa City law office was a crumbling, adobe building standing by itself on a littered, weed-grown lot. The sign over the door hung askew, supported by one rusting nail. It looked like an abandoned relic and, inside, it was worse.

The building was longer than it was wide and divided into two rooms; the front room was the law office, an untidy place littered with several empty whiskey bottles and the remnants of old meals on tin plates. Flies buzzed busily in and out through a broken window pane, and the strong odor of garlic and chili hung like a repellant miasma in the room.

Sheriff Breller surveyed the place with choking distaste. A man snored loudly in the cell just behind the battered desk. He was sleeping on a straw pallet under the one barred window. The cell door was open.

"Cripes!" Windy said and turned to look at the lawman. "Get me out of here, sheriff! I'll take the rope anytime —"

Breller walked into the cell, grabbed the sleeping man by his whiskers and yanked. The deputy came up with a howl, clawing at the air.

Breller said: "Goddamit, Slim, I'd fire yuh if I could find somebody who'd work for the pay yo're getting!"

Slim rubbed his whiskers. "Jist takin' a li'l nap, sheriff. Wasn't expectin' yuh."

"I can see that!" Breller snapped. He turned to the men standing behind Jim and Windy. "Bring them in here!"

Windy hung back, protesting. Sheriff Breller was in no mood to sympathize. They were rudely shoved inside, the iron-barred door slammed shut and locked.

Strauss said angrily: "Yo're makin' a mistake, sheriff. These men —"

"Don't tell me what to do, Strauss!" the sheriff interrupted him coldly. "I run the law in this county, even if I don't get down into Mesa City as often as I want!"

He eyed the Diamond L foreman, a cold glint in his gray eyes. "And I've been doing a little riding around myself," he said. "I'm not so sure these men are behind all the trouble here."

Windy said: "You're right, sheriff. We're jest innocent strangers, riding through —"

"Shut up!"

Long Jim pulled Windy back from the cell door. The sheriff turned back to his deputy.

"I want this pigsty cleaned out before suppertime. And keep an eye on the prisoners. Think you can manage that?"

Slim Packer drew himself up to his five foot ten of physique-less height. The effort brought on a fit of coughing.

"Ain't nobody gonna get them out of my sight, sheriff!" he promised.

The sheriff shook his head and went outside.

VI

Mal Oysterling was starting to clean up when Box-Ear stamped into the saloon, ignoring the CLOSED sign nailed to the door. The Diamond L foreman was in sour mood. The big saloonkeeper turned the job over to his swamper and he and Strauss went for a private talk in his back room.

"Damn meddlin' sheriff!" Strauss growled.

Oysterling went to a small cupboard and poured drinks from a private bottle. The room was small, cluttered with odds and ends, and ventilation was through a small window opening to an alley. Oysterling figured his accounts here. Various bills, some of them years old, were stuck on nails on the wall around his desk.

Oysterling handed Box-Ear his drink and touched his swelling eye. He could barely see the Diamond L foreman in the deepening gloom.

"You know them two old wildcats?"

Strauss nodded. "Ran into them once, up in Montanny. I was doing a little brand blotting." He scowled. "I owe them plenty."

"Think they killed Cheeky, Card an' Sturgeon?"

"Mebbe. Not that I give a hang," Strauss growled. "Found out the three of them were doublecrossing us — branding V Bar cows and selling them down in Chihuahua!"

Oysterling shook his head. "Gettin' so's a man can't trust anybuddy," he said, morosely. "Not even yore feller rustlers."

The dusk was thickening in the room and he got up and lighted a lamp.

"Hendricks is due in day after tomorrow. How many head we got for him?"

The Diamond L foreman considered. "Five hundred, more or less. Some V Bar beef, rebranded. Rest of them Diamond L."

Oysterling sipped his drink. "At the prices he gives us, and the payoff to yore boys, that doesn't leave us much." He shook his head moodily. "When I came into this with you I figgered we'd make a quick killing, then light out for some place in Mexico . . . Vera Cruz, mebbe, or Tampico . . . an' live high off the hog."

Box-Ear shrugged. "I like it fine right here, Mal. I got a boss who doesn't bother me at all. Let's me run the spread." He leaned back, grinning. "Cripes, I'm stealin' him blind an' he's out grouse huntin' —"

"Alone?" Oysterling's swollen eye narrowed as a thought hit him.

"Far as I know," Strauss said, nodding. "Takes his house boy, Ah Fong, along. Calls him his gun bearer. Packs a tent, a case of Scotch, an' a fryin' pan. Hell, he's gone so much of the time I got trouble remembering what he looks like."

Oysterling said flatly: "Let's kill him!"

Strauss shook his head. "Thought of that. But not with Sheriff Breller around. 'Sides, his brother's a duke or earl or somethin' in England. . . . Be a stink around here if somethin' happened to him."

Oysterling looked disappointed. "Then let's clean him out. You said he'd never know the difference. Blame it all on the V Bar."

"We got to get rid of Breller first," Strauss growled. "He's beginnin' to nose around too much."

Oysterling touched the swelling under his eye again. "What about them two thet busted up my place?"

Box-Ear frowned. His humiliation by them in front of his men was still a sore spot with him.

"If the sheriff hadn't stopped us they'd be hung now!" he growled.

Oysterling scratched the tip of his nose. "I got an idea," he said. He began to chuckle. "We let them go —"

Strauss stared at him. "You crazy?"

"Like a fox," Oysterling grinned. "Look, we want to get rid of Sheriff Breller. Right? We let them make a jail break tonight. Sheriff Breller takes off after them. He winds up with a bullet in his back." He leaned back in his chair, eyeing Box-Ear. "Chasin' fugitives is a risky business. An' Breller's been steppin' on too many toes around here for anybody to care much . . ."

" 'Cept his widow," the Diamond L foreman muttered. It had not been his idea, so he was reluctant to accept it. "What about those two old buzzards in jail?"

"You'll be in the posse with Breller," Oysterling said. "You find them after they kill the sheriff an' you hang 'em. Right off."

He chuckled. "Can't lose, Strauss."

Box-Ear poured himself another drink. "Won't be easy, with Breller in town. An' he's got Slim so scared that damn deppity's ready to shoot at shadows."

"Leave it to me," Oysterling said. "I got just the man to do the job for us."

Box-Ear watched the huge saloonkeeper

walk to the door and look out into the bar room.

"Useta be the smoothest con man in El Paso, in the old days," Oysterling said. "Slicked me outa two thousand pesos once . . . that was when two thousand pesos were worth a lot more than they are now."

Box-Ear joined him in the doorway. He eyed the swamper working in the far corner of the room.

"Him?" There was vast skepticism in the remark.

Oysterling nodded. "Leave Slim to me. We'll have those two old rustlers out of jail before midnight."

Strauss shrugged, not wholly convinced. "I'll be over at Maggie's," he growled. "Haven't checked in with her since I heard she got in a new girl."

Oysterling walked to the door with him and let the Diamond L foreman out. Then he turned and eyed the swamper. The man was surreptitiously sweeping debris under a table in the far corner of the room. He was a long, thin man of indeterminate age with whitish blond hair long on his neck. His clothes had long since seen better days.

He was working with his right arm pressed in close to his threadbare coat, as though he had a crippled hand.

"Reeves!" Oysterling bellowed.

The thin man looked startled. He leaned on his broom, blinking.

"Dammit! Come here!"

Reeves shuffled resignedly toward the saloonkeeper. Oysterling waited until he was close, then his right hand shot out and grabbed the swamper by the throat while he slipped his left under Reeves' coat, catching the bottle of whiskey before it slipped to the floor.

Reeves' face began to turn purple. He spluttered helplessly.

Oysterling released his grip and hauled him, wobblykneed and unresisting, into the back room and closed the door.

"How many times," Oysterling growled, "have I warned you about stealing my whiskey?"

Reeves rubbed his throat where the marks of the saloonkeeper's powerful fingers were still visible.

"What whiskey?"

Oysterling held up the bottle. "This whiskey!"

Reeves drew himself up and carefully adjusted his frayed string tie.

"Mr. Oysterling, that's your whiskey!"

The big man's face congested. "Dammit!

I know it is!" He waved the bottle in front of the swamper's nose. "Where does it belong, Reeves?"

The thin man glanced toward the bar room. "On a shelf behind the bar." He shook his head. "But I imagine that a man of your stature and incorruptible honesty, Mr. Oysterling, can steal his own whiskey if he so chooses. I am but a humble employee. I have no right to question you."

"Question *me?*" Oysterling grabbed Reeves by his coat lapels and shook the man until Reeves' teeth rattled. "Dammit, it was you who stole —"

"Tut, tut, Mr. Oysterling. You have the bottle of whiskey in your hand, not I. However, if you wish to insist that I stole it, I can only bow to your judgement, as a slave bows to the will of his master."

Oysterling staggered back toward the small table where he and Box-Ear had been drinking and sat down. He was a crafty man with his own brand of crooked logic. But verbal gymnastics such as Reeves used left him confused.

"Sit down," he said.

Reeves slipped into a chair.

"I have a job for you."

Reeves studied the saloonkeeper, his pale eyes direct and disconcerting.

"I already have a job, Mr. Oysterling."

Oysterling put a huge fist under the smaller man's nose. "Shut up an' lissen!"

Reeves' eyes wavered. "May I have a drink from your bottle, Mr. Oysterling?"

The saloonkeeper shoved the bottle toward him. "One drink."

Reeves uncorked it and tilted the bottle to his mouth. His Adam's apple didn't move, but an amazing amount of whiskey began to gurgle down his throat.

Oysterling snatched the bottle away from him.

"I want you sober, you idjit!"

Reeves wiped his mouth with the back of his hand.

"How well do you know Breller's deppity, Slim?"

Reeves frowned. "We're old drinking buddies."

Oysterling said: "Wait here." The big man went out into the bar room and Reeves eyed the bottle on the table in front of him. But Oysterling returned before he could summon enough courage to reach for it.

Oysterling placed two bottles of cheap rotgut on the table in front of Reeves.

"What's that for?"

"I want you to make a present of them to Slim."

Reeves licked his lips. "Both bottles?"

Oysterling nodded.

"What's the occasion?"

"Hell, I don't care," Oysterling growled. "You think of something."

Reeves eyed the big saloonman. "You want something from Slim, Mr. Oysterling?"

"Yeah. I want him dead drunk before midnight!"

Reeves stared at him. "Why?"

"Soft-hearted, that's all!" Oysterling snapped. "What in hell you care why?" He stuck his thick forefinger under Reeves' nose.

"I want Slim so likkered up he won't remember what he did. Then you take his cell keys and turn those two old codgers loose. After that you come back here and I'll let you steal a bottle of whiskey from my private stock."

Reeves stroked his chin, his eyes thoughtful. "Appears mighty risky, Mr. Oysterling. Sheriff Breller is a most hardnosed lawman. And I'm not on the best of terms with the law, as you know —"

"Look," Oysterling interrupted harshly, "the sheriff will think Slim did it. Slim will be so drunk he won't know for sure if he let them out or not. And I'll swear you were in here with me all the while this was going on. Everybody knows Slim's a liar, anyway."

Reeves reached for the open bottle of whiskey. Oysterling slammed his palm down on his hand.

"*After* you come back!"

Reeves got to his feet and slipped the bottles under his coat.

"It'll be a pleasure," he said.

VII

Windy Harris walked to the cell door and eyed the man cleaning up the office.

"Hey!" he said wrathfully, "there's only one bunk in here!"

Slim paused, leaning on his swab. He frowned. "So?"

"There's two of us," Windy reminded him. "How do you expect us to sleep?"

Slim grinned. "One at a time, Pop." He chuckled at his sudden wit. "Never had more than one drunk in there at a time."

Windy failed to see the humor of it. He pointed to Long Jim sprawled on the bunk.

"It's illegal, deppity."

"What's illegal?"

"One bunk — two prisoners." Windy shook his head. "Reckon you'll have to let one of us out."

Slim eyed the pint-sized oldster for a moment. "Wise galoot, eh?" he growled. He started swabbing the floor again.

Long Jim swung his legs off the bunk and joined Windy at the cell door.

"When do we get fed?" There was a

wistful eagerness in Long Jim's voice.

Slim ignored him.

Long Jim rattled the door. "Hey! The law says you got to feed prisoners."

Slim paused, eyed the long-shanked oldster with frowning regard.

Windy grinned. "Let me out an' feed him. That's the law!"

Slim slowly set his swab aside, walked to the gun rack and took down a double-barreled shotgun. Windy and Long Jim eyed him in sudden alarm.

"Hey!" Windy said.

Slim walked to the desk, took a box of shells from a desk drawer and slipped the loads into the shotgun chambers. Snapping the barrels into place, he leveled the shotgun at the two prisoners.

"This is the law," he said calmly. "You want to argue the case?"

Windy bristled. "Why, you addle-pated nitwit —"

He choked on his words as Slim cocked both hammers. Long Jim hastily pulled his partner away from the door.

"The damn fool might just do it," he muttered.

Both men sat disconsolately on the bunk. Slim laid the shotgun down on the desk and continued swabbing.

Long Jim eyed his partner. "You an' yore damn celebrating. If we'd'a been eating 'stead of drinking, we'd never have gotten into this mess."

Windy gave him a disgusted look and reached in his pocket for the makings. He found tobacco but no papers and took out his corncob pipe instead. The cracked stem was held together by strips of rawhide. He used this sparingly, for the bowl had built up a powerful residue through the years and Long Jim generally moved twenty yards upwind whenever he smoked it.

Long Jim shuddered as Windy lighted up. "Cripes," he muttered. "Not in here!"

"Change the air a bit," Windy said, puffing contentedly.

Long Jim walked to the lone barred window and looked out onto an alley. It was dark outside. The various sounds of Mesa City intruded on the night . . . barking dogs, someone yelling at his wife, someone playing a guitar. Loud voices raised in sudden anger. Some laughter.

No one gave a hang about the two of them in jail, Long Jim reflected morosely. No one cared.

The door opened and the sheriff came inside. Slim glanced at him, startled, then started swabbing vigorously.

Sheriff Breller eyed him for a moment, "I thought I told you to keep this door locked," he growled.

Slim nodded. He didn't remember the sheriff telling him this, but he did not dare to contradict the lawman.

The sheriff jerked a thumb toward the door. "Go get yourself something to eat. I'll keep an eye on them."

Slim set his swab against the wall. Breller, walking to the desk, eyed the shotgun. "What's this for?"

Slim was putting on his hat. "Pacifier, sheriff. That li'l one was talkin' too much. Tryin' to bamboozle me with some legal trickery."

"That ain't hard to do," Breller said unkindly. He waited until Slim reached the door and then said: "I said eat, Slim — not drink! I'm going to smell yore breath when you get back!"

Slim bobbed his head in agreement. "Nary a drop, sheriff. I promise."

The sheriff sighed. "Get back here in fifteen minutes!"

He checked over some old, unopened mail after Slim departed and went through a stack of dodgers. He seemed surprised not to find any that answered to the description of his two prisoners.

Windy wandered back to the cell door. "Sheriff," he said earnestly, "you got the wrong men locked up here. Box-Ear's the man you should have."

"You know Clem Strauss?"

Windy's jaw dropped. "Clem? That his name?"

The sheriff shrugged. "Name he gave when he hired on at the Diamond L."

"Met him once, up in Montanny," Windy said. He turned to his partner. "You ever hear him called Clem?"

Long Jim shook his head. "Heard him called a lot of other things, though," he growled. He joined Windy at the cell door. "Horsethief, rustler. There was even a rumor he hung out with the Hole-In-The-Wall gang."

The sheriff seemed uninterested. He picked up a piece of correspondence, shook his head, crumpled it in his fist and threw it into the wastebasket.

Windy said: "You still looking for Miguel's ghost?"

Breller's head jerked up at this one. His eyes narrowed.

"What do you know about Miguel?"

"We spent a night at the Fervans spread," Windy replied. "Someone shot up the place while we were there, tossed a note through the window. Claimed he was Miguel's ghost."

"Miguel's dead," Breller said harshly. "I killed him!"

"Then it's his ghost," Windy snapped. "Or his sister."

Breller stood up and walked to the cell. "Maria?"

Windy and Long Jim exchanged glances. "That's her name. She and Lincoln Fervans' boy have teamed up to drive the Fervans off their place."

Breller frowned. "I've been looking for her since I heard Maria had come back from Mexico City." His tone sharpened. "What's this about Wally Fervans?"

Windy shrugged. "Ran into them day before yesterday. Right after leaving the V Bar. We was on our way south, sorta looking things over."

He felt Long Jim's fingers tighten warningly on his arm and his voice trailed off. "Least I *think* it was the Fervans boy, sheriff."

"It was!" Breller snapped. "Damn fool kid, running around with that de Santoro girl! I told him —"

He turned as Slim came inside. The deputy hung his hat on a hook, walked to the sheriff and blew in his face. He beamed expectantly.

"For cripe's sakes!" Breller growled, shoving him away. He jerked a thumb toward the prisoners as he walked to the door.

"Keep an eye on them," he ordered. "I'm taking them to Connorsville in the morning to stand trial!"

The night wore on, quieter than usual — for the inhabitants of Mesa City were aware that Sheriff Breller was in town and the sheriff brooked no nonsense.

Slim dozed in his chair, his feet propped up on the desk, his hat over his eyes. His snores were muffled. At intervals they stopped altogether and he lay still, like a man who had just died. Then a tremor would run through his body, his chest would cave in as he sucked in air, then his snoring would start all over again.

Long Jim lay on the cot, trying to get some sleep. Windy prowled restlessly around the small cell, pausing every so often by the barred window facing the alley. The anesthetic whiskey had provided had faded. All the bruises he had picked up in the bar room brawl seemed accentuated now. His tongue kept probing at his loosened tooth.

He turned as someone knocked hesitantly on the door.

Slim's snores drowned it.

Whoever was outside waited a moment, then decided to put more emphasis into it. The first rattled the flimsy door panels.

Slim awoke with a jerk. His hat slid to the floor as he put his hand on his shotgun.

"Yeah?"

Reeves' voice said quickly: "Open up, Slim."

Slim turned to face the door. He seemed surprised, but not displeased. "That you, Reeves?"

"Damn it, open up!"

Slim went to the bolted door, but he was uneasy, remembering Breller's warning.

"What do you want?"

"Cripes!" Reeves snarled, "you gonna leave me out here all night?"

Slim slipped the bolt back and swung the door open. Reeves stepped inside. He was hugging the two bottles of whiskey under his coat.

"Shut the door!"

Slim complied. His eyes widened as he saw Reeves place the bottles on the desk and involuntarily his tongue licked across his lips.

"What's that for?"

"Celebration." Reeves grinned. "Yore birthday, you damn fool!"

Slim scratched his head. "My birthday?"

"Didn't you say you were born in July?"

Slim frowned. "Some time in the summer —"

Then, turning fearfully toward the closed door. "If Breller should walk in here now —"

"He's asleep," Reeves reassured him. "I heard him tell the desk clerk to wake him at sunup."

He uncorked a bottle.

Windy said: "Need help with that?"

Both men ignored him.

Slim said uneasily: "Jest a nip, Reeves."

He took the bottle and downed a generous fifth of it. He handed it back to Reeves. Reeves hesitated. "Come on," Slim growled. "I ain't gonna drink by myself."

They were down to the last third of the second bottle and beginning to slur their words when someone rapped on the door.

Reeves paused, alarm in his eyes.

Slim choked on his swallow. He looked wildly around for a place to hide the bottle. His voice came as through a wringer: "Jest a minnit, sheriff —"

But the voice that reached through the

closed door was that of a girl.

"You want have some fun, hah? Me, Conchita . . ."

Reeves let out a sigh of relief.

Slim said angrily: "Go away!"

Windy had his back to the barred window, watching the goings on in the office. A pebble sailed through the window and landed by his feet.

He turned to look irritatedly at Long Jim sitting up on the cot.

"What in hell you doing?"

"Doin?" Long Jim shook a fist at his partner. "Why, you pint-sized galoot —"

Both men stilled as someone just outside the barred window hissed.

Windy shot a look to the office. Slim was still arguing with the girl outside.

"I said I wasn't interested, Conchita. Now damn it, get out of here!"

Long Jim paced to the cell window. Wally Fervans was in the alley shadows outside. He handed a gun up to Long Jim, through the bars.

"Your horses are saddled and waiting in back. Hurry up 'fore some fool stumbles by this way!"

He ducked out of sight down the alley. Long Jim slipped the Colt inside his shirt. Someone whistled outside.

It was the signal the girl was waiting for. She said: "Beeg Americano lover, hah!" She moved away from the law office.

Slim walked back to his desk. He was frightened. And suddenly sober. "I've had enough celebratin'," he told the swamper. "You better get out of here, Reeves."

"Just one more for the road," Reeves said. He was wondering how he could get past Slim to the key ring on the wall. He knew he couldn't go back and face Oysterling with the prisoners still in their cell.

Long Jim called: "Hey, deppity!"

Slim grabbed his shotgun, turned to the cell. "You shut up!" he said. He had just enough liquor in him to be dangerous.

Windy eyed his tall partner, not understanding what was going on.

Long Jim held up a twenty dollar gold piece. "Twenty pesos, American. It's yores for a decent meal."

Slim said to Reeves: "Get moving." He walked to the cell door with his shotgun. "Lemme see that."

Reeves cursed. "Slim —"

Slim swung the shotgun around. "I said get out, Reeves! I've had enough celebratin'!"

Reeves shrugged sullenly and went to

the door; he slipped the bolt back and suddenly backed up as a slim Mexican girl jammed a cocked Colt under his ribs.

Maria walked in with him. Slim stared in frozen horror for a moment, then turned as Long Jim stuck his Colt through the bars.

"Drop it, Slim!"

Slim hesitated, dreaming nightmares of what Breller would do to him in the morning. Better suicide —

He started to swing the shotgun muzzles around. Long Jim snaked an arm through the bars and grabbed him by the back of his neck and jerked the deputy against the bars.

The shotgun blasted a hole in the ceiling. Reeves dropped to the floor and rolled under the desk, cowering.

Maria turned the Colt on Slim. Long Jim snapped: "No shooting, Maria!"

He grabbed the shotgun away from Slim, shoved him away from the cell door.

Wally Fervans came running in from the street, a gun in his hand. "Holy hell!" he snarled at Windy and Long Jim, "can't you even break out of jail without making a fuss?"

Slim sat down on the floor and began to sob.

Maria stepped over him and grabbed

keys from a hook above the desk and opened the cell door. Long Jim and Windy paused just long enough to snatch up their hardware, then went out the door with Wally and the girl.

Some men were converging cautiously toward the jail. Wally snapped several shots in their direction and the shadowy figures disappeared abruptly.

The horses were waiting in back of the jail, as Wally Fervans had said. The four of them rode out of Mesa City two minutes later. . . .

VIII

Sheriff Breller eyed the man in the cell without compassion.

"You can rot in there, far as I'm concerned!"

He turned and glared at the men crowding inside the law office. "I want him fed once a day — bread and water! Anybody who slips him anything stronger will answer to me!"

Slim clutched at the cell bars. "I wasn't drunk, sheriff! Sure, I had a few drops . . ." He shrank back as the sheriff swung around to him. "Look, sheriff . . . Reeves was in here with me. He can back me up. There was two of them who busted in here — a Mex gal an' a young feller —"

"Reeves?" The sheriff waggled a finger under Slim's nose. "Who's he?"

"Swamper in the Black Arrow Bar. Works for Mr. Oysterling."

Mal Oysterling shook his head as Breller gave him a look. "He's dreaming, sheriff. Reeves was in my place, cleaning up, when the jail break took place."

"He's lyin'!" Slim screamed. "Reeves was right in here with me! Ran out when —"

Breller held up the empty whiskey bottles. "What about these?"

"Reeves brought them," Slim admitted. "For my birthday. We jest had a nip or two."

The sheriff hurled the bottles into the wastebasket. "Bread and water!" He snarled as he herded the onlookers outside. "I'll hang the first man who brings him anything else while I'm gone!"

He closed and locked the door on Slim Packer's wails of distress.

Box-Ear waited as Sheriff Breller ordered the curious to go on home.

"Ain't you going after those two killers, sheriff?"

Breller fixed him with a cold stare. "You good at tracking at night?"

Box-Ear scowled. "No, but —"

"Then shut up!" Breller said ungraciously.

Box-Ear stiffened, his tone hard and resentful. "I'm only trying to help. I've got a half dozen men I can get into saddle in ten minutes —"

The sheriff cut him off. "Ain't anything I can do now," he growled. "I'm going to bed."

"They could be in the next county by sunup."

"They could." Breller's voice was indifferent.

Box-Ear scowled. "All right," he said harshly, "yo're the law. But you ain't Gawd! Them two old buzzards have been rustling Diamond L beef. An' they probably killed three of my men. I don't give a hang what you do, sheriff — but if I find them anywhere in the county, I'm gonna hang them!"

He turned on his heel and stalked off. Mal Oysterling gave the sheriff a worried look.

"Can't blame him for being mad, sheriff?"

Breller shrugged.

Oysterling watched him stride back to the hotel, then he followed the Diamond L foreman to the bar.

The BLACK ARROW was dark. Reeves had gone into hiding somewhere. A dim glow burned in Oysterling's back room.

Neither man who entered it was in good mood. Things had not gone well for Box-Ear and Oysterling.

The big saloonman growled: "He's a stubborn man, the sheriff. And I don't like the way he's taking this. 'Pears to me Breller knows more than he's been lettin' on."

Strauss plucked at his right earlobe. "Dammit, I figered to have some of my men riding with him. But if he's going to ride out alone —"

"Wait a minnit," Oysterling said, frowning. "Mebbe it'll still work out the same. Breller will be trailin' two escaped prisoners. Desperate men. Anythin' can happen —"

Box-Ear nodded. "I'll send Indian Joe. He's the best tracker in the county — an' he'll cut anybody's throat for five pesos."

He emptied the bottle of whiskey into his glass. "With Sheriff Breller out of the way, we'll strip the Diamond L clean. An' with Crail Hendricks frontin' for us, we'll be able to pick up the V Bar for a song."

Oysterling lifted his glass. "With Lincoln Fervans' own money."

Both men felt suddenly good, contemplating this. They drank a toast to visions of sudden wealth.

The moon rose late over the hills, a wobbly red orb that cast a sullen and angry glow over the ragged border hills.

The four riders topped a slope and looked down at the pale gleam of a river sliding past below.

Mexico lay beyond, as empty and inhospitable as the land behind them. A small wind rustled among creosote, bringing with it the lonely and desolate cry of a hunting hawk.

Windy shifted his weight in saddle. The feel of his Frontier snugged in its holster made him feel good. His head was clear. His bones ached, but he was used to a little discomfort.

He started to say: "Mighty grateful to you —"

But he closed his mouth abruptly as he found himself looking into Maria de Santoro's rifle muzzle.

"Just keep riding," she said. There was no friendliness in her voice. "If I see you or your partner in this part of the country again you'll be shot!"

The gall of this young woman was too much for Windy. He started to splutter, but Long Jim's voice overrode him.

"Ma'am," Long Jim said drily, "that's no way to speak to yore elders."

"I speak what I want," she said coldly. She made a slight motion with the rifle. "Go!"

Long Jim ignored her. He turned to the youngster slouching in his saddle.

"You let her do your talking for you?"

Wally grinned. "Maria's a headstrong

girl," he admitted. "And right now she has a grievance, grandpa."

"Lots of people have grievances," Long Jim cut in grimly. "We have one right now."

Maria said ominously, "I will not listen to further talk. It was not my idea to get you out of jail. And if you don't start riding —"

"Easy, Maria . . . easy." Wally's tone was placating. "They're going." He turned to face Windy who had gone dangerously silent.

"Reckon this squares it, grandpa?"

"I ain't yore grandpa!" Windy snapped testily. "If I was I'd give yuh a hiding!" He turned to Maria. "And you put that rifle away before I take it from you and turn you over my knee!"

The girl quivered with sudden outrage. "You'll . . . *what?*"

Wally slapped her rifle muzzle up as she fired. Long Jim kneed his horse in close, twisted the rifle from her grasp. Wally then reached for his holstered gun, but paused as Windy's right hand came up, holding a long-barreled Frontier under his nose.

"The name's Harris!" Windy said harshly. "Mister Harris to you! And this human beanpole is Mister Evers! Think you can remember that?"

Wally's eyes narrowed angrily. "Yeah." Then, bitterly, "Maybe I should have let Maria shoot you!"

The girl gave him a condemning look. "I told you all gringos are not to be trusted!"

She held out her hand to Long Jim, her manner and tone imperious . . . it was obvious she was used to having her own way.

"Mister Evers, I want my rifle back!"

He eyed her, only partially amused by her effrontery. "Promise — no shooting?"

She nodded. He handed her the rifle. She immediately backed her horse away, leveled the muzzle at Long Jim.

"Fools, too," she sneered. "Two old fools."

She turned to young Fervans. "And you — you're a bigger fool than both of them!"

She whirled her mount around and rode off toward the river.

Wally looked disgruntled. "Now see what you did!"

Windy stared at him. "What *we* did?"

"Made her mad at me." Wally shook his head. "I should have left you in jail to hang."

"Kid," Long Jim began sadly, "appears

to me you've got yore loyalties mixed up. You should be home helping yore ma and pa, 'stead of chasing around after that fire-eating, spoiled Mexican gal."

Wally scowled. "That spoiled Mexican gal is going to be my wife! That is, if you two old buzzards quit sticking your noses into what is none of your business!"

"Boy," Long Jim intoned solemnly, "you marry that gal an' you won't need anybody else to give you a mess of troubles."

Windy said: "How'd you know we was in Mesa City?"

"The de Santoros have friends all over this part of the country," Wally snapped. "There isn't anything goes on she and her brother don't know about."

Windy glanced at his partner. "You mean Miguel, Kid?"

Wally nodded.

Long Jim scowled. "The sheriff said he killed him."

"Shot him," Wally admitted. "Nearly died. He was fished out of the river . . . been a year recovering. He'll never be well again. He's . . . like my pa . . . crippled. But he's hanging on, waiting for the day when he gets back his ranch. He wants to be buried there."

"And yo're helping him?"

"The V Bar belongs to the Santoros," Wally snapped. He pointed eastward. "You saved my skin the other day. Now Maria and I have saved yours. Why don't you two be reasonable and mosey on, while you have a chance. Maria means what she says. She hates gringos. Next time she spots either of you she'll start shooting . . ."

He pulled his horse around. "And you know what Box-Ear will do, if he runs into you!"

He dug his heels into his horse's flanks and the animal leaped ahead. He rode fast after Maria who was a distant figure splashing across the river far below.

Long Jim eyed Windy, who was slowly sliding his Colt into his holster.

"Looks like we ain't wanted around here," he commented drily. "Mebbe we better do like the Kid said . . . ?"

Windy frowned. "I don't like being chased out of the country by a girl, even if she is a mighty pretty one. 'Sides, I was thinking about a man in a wheelchair. Being stole blind by Diamond L rustlers, an' them sloppy runnin' iron artists at that!" He shook his head. "A helpless man, Jim . . . being driven off his spread by a smart-alecky girl an' his own son."

The small man pondered this for a while

and Long Jim sighed, knowing the outcome of Windy's thinking.

"Wal," he said judiciously, "let's get going. Might be we kin make it back to the V Bar in time for supper . . ."

IX

The sun was slanting down behind the trees that shaded the V Bar when the two running iron samaritans rode up.

There was a loaded wagon waiting in front of the ranchhouse. Lincoln Fervans sat stiffly on the seat, his hands gripping the sides. The redheaded foreman, Rolly, was tightening the cinch straps of his mount a few feet away.

Rolly turned quickly as he heard them ride into the yard. He jerked his rifle free of its saddle scabbard and swung the muzzle around to target them.

Windy pulled up a few yards away, leaned over his saddle horn and spat tobacco juice over his dun mare's ear. His glance slid over the wagon bed, held briefly on the two hidebound trunks and the bulging carpetbag. The wheelchair was piled on top of these and lashed down.

"Bad time to be travelin'," he said.

"Cooler," Rolly replied. He looked toward the house as Lucy Fervans appeared in the doorway. "And safer."

The woman eyed them, a small light of pleasure flickering in her eyes. She was carrying a small handbag.

Windy looked at her. "Fine spread," he said. "Too bad yo're leaving."

Lincoln Fervans turned stiffly toward them. "Don't have a choice," he said harshly. "You were here the other night —"

Lucy came down the steps and paused by the wagon. She looked at the two oldsters, then up to her husband. A ray of hope glimmered in her eyes.

"Lincoln," she said, "maybe we —"

He cut her off. "Get aboard, Lucy!"

Long Jim said: "We know how you feel, Mr. Fervans. But maybe yo're being a mite hasty. It ain't Saturday yet . . ."

Lincoln shrugged. It was an effort for him to sit there on the seat. He was helpless and it galled him.

"There's some food in the cupboards," Lucy said, nodding toward the house. "You're welcome to it."

"Thank you, ma'am." Long Jim exchanged glances with his partner.

"Yore son's back," Windy said. "We ran into him the other day."

Lucy's eyes brightened. "Walter?"

Windy nodded.

Lucy turned to her husband. "You hear

that, Lincoln? Walter's come back."

Lincoln's face was stony, unyielding. "Is he? I don't see him!"

"He'll be here!" Lucy turned to Windy. "Won't he?"

Windy shifted uncomfortably in saddle. "Wal, not exactly, ma'am. Seems like he's still feeling mad about something."

The disappointment in her face hurt Windy.

"He's a bit headstrong," she said, her lips quivering. "But he'll be back. I always knew he would." She looked up at her husband again. "Soon as he gets over feeling sorry for himself, Lincoln."

She looked at Windy. "Did you . . . did you tell him about his father?"

Windy nodded. "I told him."

"Lincoln . . . let's wait!" Her face was aglow with hope. In the fading light she looked younger than Windy remembered.

The hardfaced man shook his head. "If he had wanted to come back he would have been here, Lucy."

His wife reached up, took hold of his arm. "Please, Lincoln . . . let's wait a little longer? He'll come home. I know he will —"

Lincoln shook her hand off his. "Come along!" He was a man used to giving orders. The bullet in his back hadn't changed him.

She sighed.

Windy said: "Wait!"

Fervans scowled.

"What are you asking for the spread?"

Lincoln eyed them, frowning, dubious. "I paid five thousand for this place," he answered. "Right now I'll take anything that's offered."

Rolly said: "Mr. Fervans —" He was suspicious of these two saddle bums and he showed it. "Yo're wastin' yore time. They probably ain't got a dime between them."

Windy was digging in his pocket. He glanced at the gold pieces in his palm, turned to his partner. "Where's that twenty you was willing to give that deppity for a meal back in Mesa City?"

Long Jim frowned, but he handed over the gold piece.

Windy rode alongside the wagon, held the money up to Fervans.

"A hundred dollars. That do it, Mr. Fervans?"

Lincoln's eyes flared. "I said I'd take the first offer. But that's ridiculous."

"Just a binder on the sale," Windy said. "We'll give you a bank draft for the rest. Forty-nine hundred dollars."

Long Jim's mouth dropped.

Lincoln said slowly: "You mean you're paying me five thousand dollars?"

Windy nodded. "We're sort of on vacation down here . . . heading down Texas way to look up my nephew. But the bank draft's good."

"Where?"

"Billings, Montana. Cattleman and Miner's Bank."

Lincoln frowned. "Be a month before I'll know whether it's worth anything."

Windy shrugged.

Lincoln's eyes narrowed. "Why are you buying the place? You know what you'll be up against?"

"Miguel's ghost?" Windy scratched the tip of his nose. "Always wanted to meet a haunt face to face."

Rolly said grimly: "Just a minnit, Pop. What if you don't come up with the rest of the money?"

"Then Mr. Fervans gets to keep the hundred — and the ranch." He looked at the man on the seat. "Ain't got a thing to lose, Mr. Fervans."

Lincoln looked down at his wife. "It's for the best, Lucy. We haven't had a decent night's sleep in weeks. We can't go on like this . . ."

Her lips trembled. "But Walter. What if he —" She turned to Windy. "He might come back —"

"We'll tell him," Windy said.

Lincoln said: "We'll need to draw up papers."

Windy shook his head. "Yore word is good enough, Mr. Fervans. Get yoreself settled first. We'll handle the paperwork later."

They shook hands on it.

"We'll be in Mesa City," Fervans told them.

Long Jim shot a look at his pint-sized partner.

Windy said: "There another town close by?"

Rolly said coldly: "There's Connorsville, the county seat."

Long Jim's voice was casual. "We don't recommend Mesa City, Mr. Fervans. Why not put up at Connorsville? We'll stop by to see you in a week or two with that bank draft."

Lincoln nodded. His wife climbed up into the seat beside him, took up the reins.

"If you should see my son . . ." she said. She was struggling to keep back the tears.

"We'll tell him," Windy reassured her. He smiled. "Don't you worry, ma'am.

95

He'll be coming around."

Something about these two men gave her hope. She felt better than she had in months as she drove off.

Rolly started to mount his bay horse.

Windy said: "Where you going?"

Rolly glanced at him. "Connorsville, probably. Look for another job." His smile was thin. "I ain't too pop'lar with the Diamond L boys these days."

"Want to stay on here?"

Rolly frowned.

"Grub an' keep," Windy said. "That's all we kin pay right now. Want to stay on?"

Rolly shook his head. "Came here with the Fervans. I don't like working for strangers."

"Look at it this way," Windy said levelly, "you'll still be working for them."

Rolly eyed them for a moment. "Sounds interesting," he admitted. "When do I start?"

Windy pointed after the wagon. "Ride along with them. See that they get settled in Connorsville."

Rolly nodded.

"If you should run into the sheriff," Long Jim interjected casually, "don't mention us."

Rolly's gaze sharpened. "Trouble?"

Windy shrugged. "Misunderstanding."

Rolly grinned. "I'll be back before Saturday night." He wheeled his bay horse around and went pounding after the distant wagon.

Long Jim looked at his partner. "That was our last hundred bucks," he said grimly. "And that talk about a bank draft —"

Windy cut him off, waving in grand gesture to the V Bar buildings. "It's ours, ain't it? Until we beat some sense into that fool kid and Miguel's ghost."

He swung down from saddle. "Mrs. Fervans said there was food in the cupboards. What are you waiting for, Jim?"

Long Jim beat him into the house by three strides.

X

Long Jim was up and foraging with the sun. When Windy awoke, the smell of frying bacon and eggs wafted to him from the kitchen. He scratched himself sleepily as he got up and joined his partner.

Long Jim pointed to the eggs. "Found 'em in the barn. Had to chase a couple of hens off, an' got myself pecked by Holy Joe."

"Holy Joe?"

"Banty rooster," Long Jim grinned. "I was poaching on his private preserve, I guess."

"Oughta be ashamed of yoreself," Windy grunted. He walked to the stove and poured himself a cup of coffee and seated himself at the table. The bullet scars were deep in the wood and the windows were all broken. In daylight the place looked run-down and battered and he thought of the slim Mexican girl who probably was the cause of all this havoc.

"Married, barefoot, an' pregnant," he muttered. "That'ud keep her outa trouble . . ."

Long Jim was coming toward the table with a panful of eggs and bacon.

He eyed his partner. "What are you mumbling about?"

"Nothing," Windy said. He waved Long Jim away with his eggs. "Coffee'll be enough for me." He shook his head. "You near cleaned out the cupboard last night. How come yo're still hungry?"

"Been hungry since daybreak," Long Jim answered. "Well," he said, eyeing the double portion of eggs and bacon, "can't let this go to waste, kin I?"

Windy watched him devour the breakfast. Out of deference to his partner, he waited until Long Jim was through eating before taking out his pipe and lighting it.

Long Jim moved closer to the open window. "One whiff from that," he observed acidly, "an' Miguel's ghost will hightail it back to wherever haunts come from."

Windy puffed unconcernedly.

"What'll we do now?" Long Jim asked, "Now that we bought ourselves a spread?"

"First thing we round up every V Bar cow we can find and bring them back here. We'll earnotch 'em and turn them loose down along the river brakes . . . closer to home and a long way from them thieving Diamond L hands."

Long Jim shrugged. "Fervans said he came here with five hundred head . . ." He scowled, looking off. "Reckon we'll have trouble rounding up a hundred."

"We can always brand us a few mavericks to make up the difference," Windy grinned.

"With Box-Ear Strauss loose in this part of the country? Lay you five to one you won't find a maverick or a sleeper inside a hundred miles of the Diamond L."

Long Jim settled back, frowning. "Wonder what kind of idjit hired Strauss in the first place?"

He finished his coffee and went to the sink, rinsing out his cup, and washing the dishes left over from last night. The sun's rays were slanting in across the yard. A bantam rooster, red and black feathered, strutted out of the barn and stopped in the yard. He drew himself up and crowed, flapping his wings.

"Yo're late," Long Jim snarled at him. "The sun's been up for an hour."

The rooster disdained reply. He walked off, strutting toward the hens coming out of the barn.

Windy put his pipe away.

Long Jim turned to him. "What we gonna do about tomorrow night?"

Windy said calmly: "Nothing."

"We gonna sit in here and let that gal take pot shots at us?"

"We won't be here," Windy said. "We'll be out there, waiting. When Maria and the Fervans boy ride up, we'll bag ourselves a coupla ghosts."

"Won't be easy," Long Jim growled. "Thet gal's got a quick trigger finger. And I ain't about to shoot a woman."

Windy bristled. "Who said anything about shooting womin? I didn't cut my eyeteeth on a rope for nothing!"

Long Jim grinned. "All right, Windy . . . you handle Maria. I'll take care of the boy."

They went outside, saddled, and rode off.

Sheriff Breller followed sign, turning south toward the Mexican border. He came to the place where the four had parted company; the tracks were more than a half day old, for Breller had wasted time in Mesa City before riding out, knowing it infuriated Strauss and thus doing it deliberately.

Now he swung away and followed two sets of tracks to a point overlooking the river and eyeing the desolate, burning land beyond. A speculative gleam sifted into his gaze.

He was a man with his own inner consistencies; he was also a man of few words and this made him dangerous.

The skin prickled at the back of his neck and he swung quickly around, his hand resting on his rifle butt . . . he saw nothing move on his back trail, but a faint warning persisted and turned his eyes cold.

He had expected to be followed. Still, it could be his imagination. A hawk soared low over the eroded land, skimming just above the sagebrush. Breller relaxed. If someone was lying out there, watching him, that hawk would have spotted him.

He sat for a moment, the sun burning through the shirt at his back. He had been sheriff in this county for ten years, and at every election his wife had urged him to quit. He had a daughter back home, almost of marriageable age, and a son topping twelve who was growing up unruly, giving his mother a hard time.

He should quit, he thought, *and take a job in town* . . . but he knew he never would.

He turned away from the river and followed Windy and Long Jim's tracks for a piece, seeing where they turned back. He was surprised at this, for he thought those two old codgers would be hightailing it out of the county.

He frowned. They could just be looking for a border crossing further down . . . but somehow he was not convinced of this.

Damn them, he thought . . . he had enough troubles without a pair of saddle bum rustlers complicating things.

He rode in a wide arc, making a show of following tracks and having difficulty picking them up. He was still not easy about someone following him.

He came upon a small mound of stones in the middle of a shallow arroyo. They had been piled there deliberately, and the top stone was flat and someone had chalked an arrow on it.

Breller studied it for a moment, then headed in the direction the arrow indicated.

It was noon when he heard the first shots. . . . They came from a thicket further on, close to the river, blasting the stillness with their reports. The sheriff pulled up and dismounted, ground-reined his cayuse, and walked back a ways, searching his back trail.

Satisfied, he remounted and rode toward the shotgun blasts, slowing as a covey of desert quail suddenly boomed into flight, veering away from him, low and fast and settling quickly to the ground beyond, scattering into the brush.

He drew his Colt and fired three quick shots into the sky. The reports banged back from the hills across the river.

Then the quiet settled down and his horse shook his head, bit-iron jingling at this foolishness from his master. Breller rode along a dry watercourse toward higher ground and eventually came to a clearing overlooking this part of the river. There was a tent pitched here, and a canvas awning stretched taut over a canvas-backed fold-up chair.

The sheriff rode up and dismounted, picketing his horse in the shade of a small gnarled tree just beyond the tent and close to two other horses and a pack mule. He returned to the tent and stood by the re-mains of a campfire, taking out a slim cigar from his vest pocket. He was puffing on it when a rangy man wearing a pith helmet strode into view, a silver-mounted expen-sive shotgun, hand-crafted in Europe, held across his left forearm. His hair was brown but his clipped military mustache had gray in it. A monocle dangled from a cord around his neck.

Behind him tagged a small Chinaman,

his pigtail knotted neatly on the back of his neck. He was carrying a brace of grouse strung on a length of cord.

Geoffrey "Tally Ho" Smythe grinned as he spotted the sheriff. He was in his forties, rawboned and tough — a man seemingly more at ease in the wilderness than in town, although he had been born into an English country manor.

"Tally ho, sheriff," he said, which was his form of greeting. His eyes were a deep, deep blue, lively and penetrating, searching Breller's face as he stuck out his hand.

"What brings you out this way, sheriff?"

Breller shrugged slightly, his eyes veiled behind his cigar smoke. "Passing by," he answered. His voice was louder than usual and his gaze slanted away from Ah Fong, to the thickets along the river.

Tally Ho waved toward his tent. "Join me, sheriff . . . a spot of Scotch and soda while Ah Fong prepares dinner . . . ?"

He was moving in close to Breller as he said this, his voice, like that of the sheriff, loud enough to carry beyond camp. As he reached the lawman his voice dropped to a quick whisper: "No one, Jim. Took a look around just before you rode up."

The sheriff relaxed slightly, nodding. "I'll take you up on the Scotch," he said loudly, "but I'll pass on the dinner."

Tally Ho went inside the tent, took a bottle of bonded Scotch from an open case, poured a generous measure in each of two glasses, added a squirt of soda water and, coming outside, handed one to Breller.

Ah Fong brought another fold-up chair for the sheriff and both men settled back in easy comfort, sipping their drink. The Scotch was warm but smooth.

Breller said softly: "Well . . . ?"

"They didn't cross the river — not here, anyway." The Englishman's voice was quiet. "Further on, perhaps." He was quiet for a few moments, and Breller sipped his drink.

"What's your loss?"

"Five hundred . . . maybe more." Tally Ho shrugged slightly. "They've been cautious so far."

"They've been stealing V Bar cows, too," Breller grunted. He sighed. "As if Fervans hasn't enough trouble already."

Tally Ho watched Ah Fong pluck the grouse. "Empty country out here," he said. "Easy to run stolen beef into Mexico."

"Your foreman's tied up with a pirate name of Oysterling," Breller said. "Town man — runs a saloon in Mesa City. Did you know that?"

Tally Ho shrugged.

"Big boss is a man name of Crail Hendricks," the sheriff added. "Looks like a preacher . . . deadly as a snake."

"Saw him," Tally Ho said. He frowned. "Rode across the river some time this morning."

"Alone?"

"Two riders — young, hard." The Englishman's eyes held a cold fire. "Gunslingers."

Breller finished his drink and Tally Ho got up and went back inside the tent to replenish it. The fly canvas over the sheriff held back the fierce beat of the border sun. But Ah Fong, squatting just beyond, cleaning the quail, took the brunt of it without complaint. He was a small, quick-eyed man clad in traditional long black jacket, voluminous sleeves, baggy white pants.

"I have enough on Box-Ear and Oysterling to jail them right now," Breller said as Tally Ho came out and handed him his drink, "but Hendricks would only find some other fools to work for him." He stretched his legs out in front of him, brooding. "I'd like to get them all in one raid — then I could turn in this badge and take things easy."

Tally Ho smiled, knowing the sheriff's

talk about resigning was just talk. He heard it every time Breller visited him.

"I'm sorry about Lincoln Fervans," he said. "This Mexican girl, the sister of Miguel." He shook his head. "You still worried about her?"

Breller's lips tightened in a bleak smile.

"You're the law," Tally Ho pointed out. "You could talk to her."

Breller shook his head. "Stubborn girl. And she stays on the other side most of the time."

He finished his Scotch. "Can't chase two things at one time, Tally Ho. But soon as we nail Hendricks."

He got up and walked to his horse. The Englishman walked with him.

"Ride easy, Jim."

Breller nodded. "Keep an eye out for Hendricks. But stay clear of him, if you can. I'll be back in a day or two."

Tally Ho watched him ride off.

It was late afternoon when Sheriff Breller reined in on a high promontory overlooking the river. The water was deep here, moving fast against the base of the hill, sliding hard and yellowish beyond, breaking into a stretch of white-water further down. This side of the river was barren, bleak . . . a thin line of green marked the Mexican side.

Somehow he almost always ended up here, Breller thought. He let his body go loose in saddle, his thoughts slipping back to the day he had finally tracked Miguel down. Here, on this bluff . . .

He was a killer, he told himself — but Miguel's dark face, turned to him that day, trapped here, was burned in his mind. He had not wanted to kill Miguel — but the young Mexican had forced it on him.

He was reaching up to his pocket for a cigar when the bullet hit him, high up in the side. He started to fall, his fingers clutching at the saddle horn. His roan reared as the rifle report slapped the stillness behind them. Breller fell, clawed himself back on his feet and made a lunge for his horse as the animal snorted and wheeled away. The second shot sent him staggering back . . . the last shot knocked him off the bluff.

Breller's roan ran wildly, stirrups flapping. It dipped into a gully and went out of sight.

The stillness flowed back over the scene. Then a man appeared, walking slowly, his rifle held easily in his hand. He was a thick-bodied man, perhaps thirty, with reddish hair over a flat, impassive Indian face. His eyes were gray. He wore a flat-crowned, black hat with an eagle feather stuck in the band, as well as a loose fitting shirt, tails hanging over black pants.

He walked to the edge of the promontory and looked down into the swirling, eddying river.

Something caught his eye. The sheriff's hat, floating, bobbing down the stretch of whitewater.

Indian Joe grunted, swung away.

His horse was picketed a quarter of a mile back, among rocks. He mounted and rode in a straight line for the Diamond L.

XI

By noon, and after much riding and cussing, Windy and Long Jim had rounded up twenty-nine head of cattle bearing the V Bar brand and turned them loose in the brakes south of the ranchhouse.

They had spotted a few more, and they guessed that, in all, fifty or sixty more steers were scattered on the range bordering the Diamond L. It would take at least a week of hard riding to flush them out of the thickets and herded south.

Long Jim wiped his forehead as he watched the last of the steers disappear into the brakes. All this work, he grumbled. And all they had wanted, coming this way, was three or four mavericks — just enough to keep them in beans and biscuits for a while.

The hundred dollars Windy had shelled out to Lincoln Fervans they had kept for emergencies.

"That's enough cow chousing for me," he said. "I'm getting hungry."

Windy headed him off. "Let's take a

look around, first. Further up the river."

They rode out again with Long Jim grumbling. A half dozen miles later they ran onto a small mound of stones in a shallow arroyo. The flat stone on top had an arrow pointing northeast.

"That's the second sign we've seen," Long Jim said. "Wonder what it means?"

"Mex, I told you," Windy replied. His tone was complacently assured.

"But what's it mean?"

Cornered, Windy fingered through his imagination. "Wal . . . it's a ghost marker, that's what it is. That's how Miguel's ghost finds his way back to the river."

Long Jim snorted. "Ghost marker! Cripes!"

He spurred on ahead, shaking his head.

Windy took out a misshapen piece of chawing tobacco, plucked some lint from it before taking a bite. He chewed on it a while, watching his partner.

They moved in the direction of the arrow and a half hour later they came within sight of a tent pitched on high ground. A pigtailed Chinaman was asleep in a chair, the smoke curls of a dying campfire rising slowly in the still air.

Long Jim glanced at his partner. "Mex, eh?"

Windy bristled. "Jest a disguise. Keep an eye on him . . . they're tricky."

They rode quietly, finally reining in less than a dozen feet from the sleeping Ah Fong. The Chinaman stirred, laughed softly in his sleep, said something in Cantonese . . . then sighed and went still again, a beatific smile on his lemon face.

Windy snickered. "All by his lonesome, dreaming of his celestial heaven. Wonder somebody hadn't roped him and cut off his pigtail."

Long Jim said loudly: "Hey, you!"

The Chinaman's eyes snapped wide open. He saw two disreputable figures looking down at him and he bounced out of his chair, chittering wildly, and dashed inside the tent.

Windy shook his head. "Now see what you've done," he chided his partner. "Scared hell outa —"

The birdshot whispered through the air above them, the tiny lead pellets kicking up little grits of granite from the rocks beyond. Both men whirled in saddle as the shotgun blast ripped the stillness.

The man coming toward them from the brush was a rangy figure dressed in bush jacket, jodphurs and pith helmet. A monocle dangled from a cord around his neck.

He walked up to them, waving excitedly.

"See it?"

Windy scowled. "See what?"

"Red-necked pheasant! Flew over this way."

"Red necked phea—" Windy choked on the words. "Ain't any pheasants in this neck of the wood, mister."

Tally Ho frowned. He placed his monocle in his left eye and studied them.

"No pheasants?" He sounded disappointed.

Both men shook their head.

Tally Ho sighed. "I was certain that I spotted one. A rare specimen, gentlemen . . . habitat, American Southwest, genus Phasianus . . . prefers arid brushy country —"

"No pheasants!" Windy and Long Jim repeated firmly. Tally Ho let his monocle drop. He shrugged, eyed the guns in their hand. "You gentlemen looking for grouse?"

Windy eyed Long Jim. Both men slipped their Frontiers back into holster.

"We're looking for the sneaky galoot who's been building little piles of stones around here."

"Stones?" Tally Ho's brow puckered. "Gentlemen, follow me. I'll show you

114

where you can pick up stones of all sizes, shapes and colors."

He started to turn back, motioning for them to follow. Windy gave up.

"Hold it, mister! We ain't in no hurry."

Tally Ho paused.

Ah Fong cautiously stuck his head through the tent flap.

Tally Ho waved to him. "My gun bearer, Ah Fong."

Windy grunted. "We met."

Ah Fong eyed both men distrustfully, fingering his pigtail.

"I was just about to have a spot of tea," Tally Ho observed. "Join me?"

"I'd rather have a spot of whiskey," Windy said.

"My pleasure," Tally Ho said. He turned to Ah Fong. "Get the water boiling, while I fix a drink for our friends."

He disappeared inside the tent while Ah Fong, with an eye cocked to the two strangers, set a small kettle on the fire.

Long Jim and Windy dismounted as Tally Ho came out of the tent with two glasses in his hands.

"I'm Geoffrey Smythe," he said, handing them the drinks. "Out here for a spot of hunting. Grouse shooting, of course."

"Of course," Long Jim parroted solemnly. He glanced at his partner. Windy was sampling the Scotch and soda. The pint-sized reprobate made a face.

"What's in this?"

"Scotch."

"What else?"

"Dash of soda water."

Windy handed the drink back to Smythe. "I don't like Scotch. And I usually drink my sarsaparilly straight."

Tally Ho looked confused.

Long Jim looked around. His tone was hopeful: "What do you usually have to eat out here?"

"Grouse," Tally Ho said promptly. Then, seeing the look on Long Jim's face: "By Jove, you're hungry." He turned to his gun bearer. "Ah Fong — see what you can prepare for my guests."

Windy started to say: "Forget it —" But Long Jim clamped a hand across his mouth. "My partner's a shy man," he explained. "Dying of starvation, and he still wouldn't say anything."

Smythe shook his head understandingly. "Remarkable man. Knew an Abyssinian like that . . . dying of thirst, he was, crossing the desert west of Khartoum. Crawling on his belly. Tongue blackened. But too proud to ask for water. Had to

116

force it on him, poor chap."

Windy cut him off. "You just passing through here?"

Tally Ho sipped the drink Windy had rejected. "You must be strangers in these parts?"

Windy and Long Jim shrugged.

"I own the Diamond L ranch," Smythe said. He saw the look that flashed into their eyes and his own narrowed and he looked away, not wanting them to see it.

"Part of my inheritance, by Jove. My father was Lord Charlton Heather Smythe of Salisbury." He screwed his monocle into his left eye again. "Sort of the black sheep of the family."

He stroked his mustache. "Served two years with the Bengal Grenadiers in India, on the Punjabi. One of the finest outfits in the British Colonial Service —"

Windy cut in weakly: "You own the Diamond L?"

Tally Ho nodded. "Have a fine chap running things for me. Gentleman name of Clemence Strauss. Possibly you've heard of him? Comes from a real fine Kentucky family, he said. He runs the ranch . . . 'spread,' he called it." Tally Ho chuckled. "Leaves me plenty of time for grouse hunting."

"I'll bet," Long Jim growled.

Ah Fong set up a small folding table and placed a platter of cooked quail on it.

Tally Ho waved to it. "Please, gentlemen . . . my pleasure."

Long Jim needed no second invitation.

Windy said: "I'll try a spot of Scotch — straight. If you don't mind, Mister," he paused, grinned. "What is it, Smythe . . . mister or Lord?"

"Call me Tally Ho," Smythe said. "Everyone else does."

He disappeared inside his tent and emerged with a generous slug of Scotch.

"A chap has to acquire a taste for it," he said, handing the drink to Windy. "A *gentleman*'s drink."

Windy raised the glass. "Mud in yore monocle, Tally Ho."

He drank the Scotch. He didn't like it, but it was better than nothing.

Smythe said: "You chaps traveling on?"

"No," Windy said. "We're neighbors of yores."

A dark and sudden look came and went in Tally Ho's eyes. "Neighbors?"

"We just bought a ranch south of here. Lincoln Fervan's spread — the V Bar."

Smythe took a big gulp of his Scotch and soda. "Well," he said finally, "I'm sorry to hear that. No offense, sir. I mean I'm sorry for Mr. Fervans. A fine gentleman. I visited him once, a few weeks after he had bought the ranch." He smiled. "Not an easy chap to get along with, though. He caught me doing a bit of grouse shooting on his land and ran me out. A bit irascible, I'd say . . . and even more so, after his unfortunate accident . . ."

"Yeah . . . you can say that," Windy nodded.

He turned to Long Jim, who was finishing his third quail. "Let's go, Jim. Be dark before we get back, if we don't get a move on."

Long Jim licked his fingers. He looked sadly at the two remaining quail. Ah Fong was shaking his head.

"Marvelous appetite," Smythe said. "Take them along, if you wish."

Long Jim hastily complied before Windy could stop him.

"By the way," Tally Ho said, watching them mount. "Say hello to the sheriff, if you run across him."

"Sheriff Breller?"

Smythe nodded. "I see you've met him. Fine chap. Stops by once in a while for a spot of tea."

The vision of the cold-eyed, tough

lawman having tea with Tally Ho Smythe was hard for them to imagine.

"We'll tell him," Windy said. He waved. "Drop in at the V Bar some time, Mr. Smythe — for a spot of grouse shooting."

Tally Ho waved back. He stood there, watching them until they rode out of sight.

Long Jim and Windy rode for a while in silence, each man occupied with his thoughts. The meeting with Tally Ho had left an indelible impression.

Finally Windy pulled aside and looked back. "Clemence Strauss," he said, and there was awe in the little man's voice. "A fine gentleman," he mimicked Tally Ho. "That's what he called Box-Ear. And he lets him run his ranch while he's out grouse shooting. Mi-Gawd!"

Long Jim frowned. "He ain't as dumb as he looks," he said. "Out here banging away at quail, sure. But what else?"

Windy eyed his partner, seeing he was serious.

"And Sheriff Breller stops by now and then," Long Jim went on. "Why?" He scratched his head. "Could be them markers are for the sheriff, eh?"

"Could be?" Windy said.

He looked back again, his eyes cold. "And we told him we bought the V Bar.

Next time the sheriff stops by —"

"We'll have the law calling on us," Long Jim growled. "Well, what the hell — can't be helped."

They rode on, the sun slanting in their faces. It had dipped below the distant hills when they came up to the V Bar.

Long Jim pulled up abruptly and laid a warning hand on Windy. Both men eyed the ranchhouse.

Two riders lounged casually in saddle — young, tough, gun-handy gents from the looks of them. A third horse, a big black stallion, was tied up by the steps.

It was the man coming out of the house, pausing on the veranda, who held Long Jim and Windy's interest.

He looked like a preacher and he dressed like one — flat-crowned black hat, long black coat, black pants, gleaming white shirt and black string tie. He looked like a pious minister come to call on sinners, and Long Jim glanced at his partner.

"Sins finally caught up with you, I see." He grinned as he said it, but his grin was cold.

Windy slid his hand casually down over his gunbutt. "Let's go see what they want, Jim."

XII

The two riders wheeled around to face them as Windy and Long Jim rode into the yard. The man in the doorway came to the head of the stairs and gave them a cold and inquiring look.

Windy said, pleasantly enough, "Looking for somebody, gents?"

The pious-faced man nodded. "We're looking for the owner of this ranch."

Windy laid his hands on his saddle within easy reach of his holstered gun.

"Yo're looking right at him, mister."

The two riders exchanged cold glances. The pious-faced man frowned.

"You Lincoln Fervans?"

"Fervans left yesterday," Windy said calmly. "I'm Mr. Harris. My partner, Mr. Evers. We bought the place from Fervans."

The tall man considered this, his piety a mask over his feelings.

"Sorry to hear that," he said. He let his gaze run disrespectfully over the two beard-stubbled, disreputable, unlikely looking ranchowners.

"You have papers, of course?"

Windy shrugged.

"I'm Crail Hendricks," the pious-looking man said. "I heard this place was for sale." He ran his gaze over the outbuildings. "Pretty rundown spread, but I could use it —"

Long Jim was eyeing the restive gunslingers. "Sorry, Mr. Hendricks," he cut in quietly, "but we ain't figgerin' on selling."

Hendricks eyed him, his anger showing now. "I've come a long way. I don't like riding this far for nothing —"

"Don't blame you," Windy said, grinning. "Looks like we beat you to it." He made a gesture for them to leave. "Sorry, gents."

Hendricks shook his head. "I'd like to see a bill of sale, before I go."

"It was a gentleman's agreement," Windy said. He was still grinning, but there was a coldness in his eyes. "Now if you all will promptly vacate the premises —"

Hendricks' hand dipped inside his coat, but his hand froze on the gun in his shoulder holster as he found himself looking into Windy's Frontier muzzle.

His two riders had dropped their hands to their gunbutts as Hendricks made his move. The taller of the two, Caswell, jerked his Colt free and Long Jim shot him, knocking him out of saddle. The other rider froze, an unbelieving look in his eyes.

Hendricks let his hand slide down empty to his side. "Pretty fast," he said coldly, "for a pair of saddle bums." He turned to the man still in saddle. "Pick him up, Frenchy," he said, motioning to the man on the ground. "He isn't hurt bad."

Frenchy dismounted warily and helped Caswell to his feet. The wounded man glared at Long Jim, his gun arm hanging limp, blood trickling down through his fingertips.

Frenchy bent down to pick up Caswell's gun.

"Leave it!"

Caswell gave Long Jim a pained, bitter look. "I'll be seeing you again, mister."

"Yore privilege," Long Jim nodded. He jerked a thumb toward the darkening road. "Now ride on out of here!"

Frenchy helped Caswell climb into saddle. He swung up beside his companion and then waited as Hendricks walked slowly down the steps and mounted his big black stallion.

Hendricks laid his hard glance on the two oldsters. "I think yo're a pair of crooks," he said bluntly. "I don't know what happened to Fervans, but I'm going to find out. And when I do I'm coming back here — with the sheriff!"

He swung his horse around and, flanked by his two men, he rode out of the V Bar yard.

Long Jim and Windy waited until they were far down the road to Mesa City, then they dismounted, led their cayuses into the barn, stripped saddle and blankets and turned them loose into stalls that opened up into a small back corral and a water trough.

They paused on the ranchhouse steps to look back toward the darkening road. Long Jim rubbed the tip of his nose, his eyes thoughtful.

"Think they'll be back, Windy?"

"Not tonight."

"Wonder if he was on the level about coming here to buy the place?"

"Mebbe."

Long Jim eyed his partner. "You thinking what I'm thinking?"

Windy grinned. "If he gets to the sheriff, we're in trouble. If he's a crook, and in with Box-Ear Strauss, it's worse . . ."

"We could grab a bite to eat and ride out tonight," Long Jim suggested, "and be in Mexico before sunup."

Windy fished in his pocket for his corncob. He was thinking of the crippled rancher and the woman who had been kind to them.

"Hell," he said slowly, "let's wait an' see what the morrow brings."

Tally Ho Smythe sprawled comfortably in his canvas chair, a Scotch and soda in his hand, and watched the sun go down over the jagged western hills. He was a man who liked being alone. He went into town only when the flesh moved him, and usually this meant a trip to St. Louis, where the bordellos were elegant and the cuisine excellent.

But most of the time he preferred being out in the "bush," as he called it. He had been a thorn of a sort in his father's side, and Lord Smythe had been glad to exile his youngest son to a cattle ranch in the American Southwest.

He had no close friends, other than Sheriff Breller, and this was a late development growing out of a common cause. Ah Fong was his only constant companion, but the Chinaman never intruded upon his privacy.

So Tally Ho rested, a lean, tough, self-sufficient man who cared very little what the people in and around Mesa City thought of him. It was the best time of day, with a breeze coming up off the river and the sun's fierce rays gone. He sat there thinking of the sheriff, and of the two strange and disreputable-looking characters who had visited his camp.

Ah Fong stirred and cocked his head and looked off toward the brush as an alien sound brushed across his reverie. Tally Ho caught the look in his camp boy's face and slowly placed his glass down beside him and reached for his shotgun.

The sound was clearer now — horse's hoofbeats. They waited, Ah Fong crouched by the campfire like a penguin, his hands hidden inside his sleeves, his slant eyes lidded and inscrutable.

The horse emerged from the brush and came toward the fire . . . it stopped, whickered tiredly at the two men. Its bit reins were dragging.

Tally Ho came out of his chair in a hurry as he recognized the animal. The big roan snorted and backed off. Its reins got tangled in a bush, holding it for a moment. Tally Ho reached him, gripping at the trailing reins.

"Easy, old chap . . . easy . . ."

He ran his gaze past the horse, into the

gathering darkness beyond and a tightness crept into his face.

Ah Fong padded up.

"The sheriff . . . ?"

Tally Ho nodded bleakly. He led the roan back to the campfire and examined the saddle. Blood had dried on the saddle skirt.

It was a dangerous game Breller had been playing, and it appeared the odds had caught up with him. Tally Ho's thoughts went back to the oldsters — neighbors of his, they had told him. New owners of the V Bar.

Tally Ho sucked in a regretful breath. He had intended alerting Sheriff Breller to this new development — now it was too late.

He glanced at Ah Fong, his eyes cold.

"We'll break camp early tomorrow," he said. "We're going visiting . . ."

Ah Fong showed him a small smile.

"The hungry one and his partner?"

Tally Ho nodded. "We'll backtrack the sheriff as soon as it gets light . . . see what we can find." He glanced off, the lines harshening around his mouth. "Then we go calling on the new owners of the V Bar."

Ah Fong smiled. "I pack tonight."

XIII

The Mexican squatted on his heels, studying the body lying face down among the reeds of the river bank. The slow current tugged at the man's legs, but the weight of the man's body, entangled in the reeds, kept him from floating away.

He was a young man, this Mexican, despite the gray in his hair, the furrows in his wasted cheeks. His right hand hung limp in his sleeve, the fingers curled slightly, locked forever in this position by severed tendons. He was wearing a charro jacket and a sheath knife hung from a belt around his waist.

Slowly and with great effort he turned the body over. Sheriff Breller's face looked up at him in the pale twilight. The lawman was still breathing. The badge on his vest was muddied.

Miguel's left hand stole to his sheath knife as he sucked in a ragged breath of surprise. For six weeks he had hovered between life and death, lying on a straw pallet in a goatherd's hut. He had survived only to find himself a cripple, and so wasted in body that a quarter mile walk left him spent and exhausted.

This man, lying here at his feet, dying . . . this was the man who had robbed him of his youth and his hopes. Even as he looked down a trickle of bright red blood frothed up and floated away on the water.

Miguel's burning glance stole away from the body, across the darkening river to the distant promontory where Sheriff Breller had caught up with him. Miguel came here often at dusk, when he was able to get around, to stand for hours gazing at that cliff, reliving that bitter day.

The sheriff stirred, and one hand reached out toward Miguel. Breller's gray eyes opened, but they were unclear. If he saw the knife in Miguel's hand it did not register. He groaned softly, and his eyes closed.

Miguel shifted slightly. He did not know who had shot the lawman, nor did he question the luck that had brought the sheriff to him. He knew only that in one quick, downward thrust of his knife he could now avenge the months of tearing pain and blasted hopes —

"Miguel!"

The voice cut sharply across the swaying

reeds, holding him. He glanced back to see Wally Fervans and his sister coming toward him.

"Time to be getting back, Miguel," Wally said, and then, seeing the body at Miguel's feet, he sucked in a sharp breath and said: "Who is it? What happened?"

Miguel said bitterly: "It's the sheriff."

Wally stood over him now, looking down at the lawman. Surprise held him speechless for a moment, then: "How'd he get here?"

Miguel shrugged. "Someone shot him — upriver, I think. He floated down here."

Maria pushed her way through the reeds to stand beside Wally. She looked down at Breller and started as the sheriff's eyes opened and he reached out a hand to her.

"He . . . he's still alive . . . ?"

"Barely," Miguel said. "But I'll make sure he does not linger."

Wally stayed his hand. "No, Miguel. He's the law. It would be murder."

Miguel eyed him resentfully. "Murder?"

Wally knelt beside him. "Yes." He took the knife from Miguel. "You know how I feel, Miguel. I'm with you and Maria all the way. But . . . but not this."

Miguel looked down on the lawman, his gaze dark and unforgiving.

"Look," Wally said, trying to reach through to this hating man, "you'll be going back to live on your ranch soon. My father is leaving. But how long will you be able to stay there, Miguel, if you kill the sheriff — ?"

"I did not shoot him," Miguel said. "I could let him die."

Wally nodded. "You could. But if we helped him — and he should live . . ." His fingers gripped Miguel's arm. "We could use the law on our side, Miguel!"

The young Mexican considered this. He was only twenty-three, but he knew he would never be strong again . . . he'd be dependent on his sister from now on, and on Wally Fervans . . .

"He shot me," Miguel said harshly. "Why would the sheriff help me now?"

Wally shrugged. "You were a fugitive. It was Breller's job. You never had a chance to tell him your story —"

"And . . . you think I have now?"

"It's worth a try."

Miguel looked at his sister. She stood cold and aloof and he could not tell where she stood.

"Well . . . ?"

Her lips curled. "*If* he lives!"

Wally looked down at the man making

clawing motions in the mud. Sheriff Breller was tough.

"Let's get him out of here," he said, "and see . . ."

The Diamond L lay backed up against a red-hued mesa, its rambling ranchhouse fanning out along its base. The main building was made of pine timbers hauled in from a sawmill in the mountains a hundred and eighty miles north.

The spread kept ten permanent riders on its payroll, not including the galley cook. Of the original Diamond L hands only he was left, a sullen, silent man name of Gant who knew well enough what was going on, but felt no compelling desire to reveal it either to the law or the ranch's new owner.

He had resented the Englishman's takeover from Shawley Brown, the original owner of the Diamond L. He felt no loyalty, therefore, to Tally Ho Smythe. But he was not crooked, and he was not part of Box-Ear Strauss' band of thieves.

It was midmorning, and most of the hands had ridden out when Gant emerged from the galley and started to empty his slop can into a drainage ditch. He paused to eye the four men who came riding into the yard. The big man with the patch over his eye he knew. He was surprised to see him, for Mal Oysterling hated to ride and seldom visited Strauss at the ranch.

The other three were strangers to the cook. At first Gant thought one of them was a minister, but he quickly put that out of his mind, cynically considering that no minister would be riding with Oysterling or come visiting Strauss.

The other two, one of them wearing a clean bandage over his upper right arm, looked familiar enough. They were like the rest of the Diamond L hands Strauss had hired — tough, gun-handy gents with few scruples. Most of them were drifters who wouldn't have been able to hold a job with any other spread.

Mal Oysterling growled at him as they rode up, "Box-Ear in?" and Gant nodded, pointing toward the house. When the English owner was away, which was often, Strauss usually made himself at home there.

The four men dismounted, and were tying up in front of the ranchhouse when Box-Ear came out to the veranda. He had a fat cigar in his mouth, and a drink in his hand. A sliver of surprise darkened his gaze as he saw them.

"Mornin', Crail —" he began, but the cold-eyed man cut him off.

"Let's go inside where we can talk!"

The four of them followed Box-Ear into a big, comfortable living room with various deer heads mounted and hanging from the walls. Caswell sprawled sullenly in a stuffed chair. Hendricks walked to the fireplace and stood with his back to it, eyeing Box-Ear, who looked uncomfortable. Oysterling fidgeted nervously. Frenchy prowled around, looking for something to drink.

Hendricks let Strauss sweat for a while, then he snapped: "I don't like being doublecrossed, Box-Ear!"

Strauss shot a look at Oysterling, and the big saloon-man licked his lips and said: "I told yuh, Crail — we didn't know —"

"Shut up!" the rustler boss snapped. "I want to hear what *he* has to say!"

Box-Ear licked his lips. "What are you talking about?"

"The V Bar!" Hendricks snarled.

Strauss was puzzled. "What happened, Crail? Fervans give you trouble?" His gaze went to Caswell. "Must have been that damned redheaded foreman, Rolly —"

"It wasn't Fervans and it wasn't his foreman," Hendricks cut in grimly. "Two men old enough to be my father. A tall beanpole and a pint-sized oldster —"

"Harris and Evers?" The names exploded from Box-Ear.

Hendricks shrugged. "They were pretty close-mouthed about who they were."

Box-Ear sagged into a chair. "What were they doing at the V Bar?"

"Said they had just bought the place from Fervans!"

Oysterling cackled harshly: "That's a damn lie, Crail! Those stumblebums didn't have enough money between them to buy a round of drinks."

Hendricks gave him a look and Oysterling gulped and shut up. The rustler boss turned his attention back to Strauss.

"Looks to me like you and this nitwit partner of yours are trying to pull a doublecross."

"Jesus!" Box-Ear snarled, jumping up. "I don't know what you ran into down there, Crail! But I swear I didn't know them two were at the V Bar!"

"You know them?"

"Sure!" Strauss said bitterly. "Knew 'em before, up in Montanny. Ran into them again, in Mesa City. Just a coupla days ago. Had both of them ready to swing from that tree in the town square. They'd be hanging there now if the sheriff hadn't stopped me!"

He ran his fingers through his thinning hair. "They broke jail the other night. I figgered they'd be in the next county by now, still riding —"

"They're not!" Hendricks said coldly. "They've taken over the V Bar."

"Where was Fervans and his wife?"

Hendricks shrugged. "I looked the place over before they showed up. Looked to me like they had moved out."

Oysterling frowned. "Mebbe those two old buzzards just moved in and took over."

"That's possible," Hendricks said. He turned to Strauss. "Where's the sheriff?"

Box-Ear glanced at Oysterling. "Dead," he said warily. "Indian Joe shot him yesterday."

Hendrick's eyes chilled. "Whose bright idea was that?"

Box-Ear stiffened. He was getting mad at being snapped at like some errand boy.

"Mine!" he said. "Goddammit, Crail, Breller was no fool. He'd been noseying around. I think he was onto us!"

Oysterling said: "We had to get rid of him, Crail!"

"Killing a lawman is bad trouble," Hendricks said.

Oysterling shrugged. "Hell, not many people around here liked Breller. Too damn strict, he was. Won't be anybody missing him — not for a long while, anyway . . ."

Hendricks paced the floor, rethinking his plans. He had figured on enlisting the law's help in ousting Harris and Evers from the V Bar.

He swung abruptly around to face Strauss.

"Who's his deputy?"

"Slim?" Then, as the Diamond L foreman sensed where Hendricks was headed, he exploded: "Christ, not *him*, Crail?"

"We'll need the backing of the law," Hendricks pointed out, when we ride down and take over the V Bar."

Box-Ear raised his eyes heavenward. "Slim Packer — the *law!* You don't know what yo're askin', Crail. Slim ain't got two cents worth of brains floating around under his skull, even sober."

"You have a better idea?" Hendricks snapped.

"Slim has an extra badge around somewhere," Oysterling said. "He deppitized Box-Ear once before. He could do it again."

Hendricks eyed the Diamond L foreman. "A badge, on *you?*" He chuckled at the incongruity of it. "Well, it might work!"

Box-Ear nodded. "It'll be legal. And this time, Crail, I'll hang them! No talk! I'll just hang the both of them from the nearest tree, right there in the V Bar yard!"

Hendricks looked around the big room. "Your boss," he said. "When's he due back?"

"Tally Ho?" Box-Ear grinned. "The Lord only knows what he does. He's out there somewhere, grouse shooting. That's all I know, Crail!"

"Round up your men," Hendricks said sharply. "I'll be in Mesa City, waiting. . . ."

XIV

Long Jim lay on his stomach, the sun slanting against his back, dark blotches of sweat showing through his shirt. He was studying the Diamond L buildings sprawled out along the base of the mesa.

"Wal, I'll be damned . . ." he muttered.

Windy crouched beside him. They were on a ridge above the Diamond L, overlooking the main road to town. They had made a swing up this way more out of curiosity than with expectancy — and four riders on the road below them had attracted their attention.

"The sheriff?" Windy said.

Long Jim handed the glasses to him. "That preacher looking feller, Hendricks. Like we figgered, he must be in with Box-Ear . . ."

Windy studied the scene below them. "That's Box-Ear, all right. They're going into the house." He set the glasses aside and scratched his head. "Don't know which I'd hate more — have the sheriff come calling on us, or Box-Ear."

"If we're smart, we'll be twenty miles in-side Mexico before nightfall," Long Jim grumbled. Then, as Windy gave him a scowling look, he shrugged. "But I reckon we ain't . . ."

Windy slid back down the slope, Long Jim following. They went to their horses, picketed in a hollow, and mounted.

It was late afternoon when they returned to the V Bar. They pulled up under the adobe archway and Long Jim suddenly put a warning hand on Windy's arm.

"Looks like we got company again."

A small curl of smoke rose from the chimney. Three horses nosed the hitchrack in front of the house. One of them was a mule, loaded down with a pack.

"Tally Ho," Windy muttered, frowning.

They rode into the yard and pulled up by the picketed animals and dismounted.

Ah Fong came to the door. He had been expecting them. He bowed, smiling. His hands were hidden inside his sleeves.

"You come back, yes . . . velly good, velly good . . ." His eyes were Oriental slits, dark and mysterious. "I fix dinner." He nodded to-ward Long Jim. "You velly hungry, no . . . ?"

Windy frowned. "Where's yore big white hunter?"

"Right here," Tally Ho said.

Both men turned. Tally Ho stood by the corner of the ranchhouse, his shotgun pointed rather carelessly at them.

"I wouldn't do that," he said sharply to Windy as the little man's hand dropped instinctively to his gunbutt. His voice was cold. "This isn't birdshot, old chap!"

Windy glanced at Long Jim. "Hell of a way to come visiting yore neighbors," he growled.

Ah Fong's right hand slipped out of his sleeve, holding a pistol. The Chinaman smiled, showing yellowish buck teeth.

"You talk peace, yes?"

Windy eyed him resentfully. "Told yuh, Jim," he muttered inconsequentially, "can't trust a man who wears a pigtail!"

Long Jim said quietly: "Easy with that shotgun, Tally Ho. It makes me nervous."

"Where's Mr. Fervans?"

Long Jim frowned. "Why?"

Tally Ho cocked the double hammers. "Just answer."

"Hell with you!" Windy cut in grimly. "We figgered that grouse shooting was just an act!" He turned to his partner. "Probably working hand in hand with his crooked foreman —"

Tally Ho cut him off. "Who shot Sheriff Breller?"

Windy and Long Jim exchanged glances. Windy said slowly: "The sheriff's been killed?"

"Appears so." Tally Ho walked closer, his blue eyes cold, angry. "You rode up right after he left my camp." The twin muzzles targeted both of them. "Which one of you shot him?"

Windy licked his lips. "Where'd it happen?"

"His horse showed up at my camp last night. I followed him back to a high promontory overlooking the river. He was shot out of his saddle while waiting there."

Windy said: "I know what you're thinking, Tally Ho. But neither one of us shot the sheriff."

Tally Ho frowned. "What do you know about my foreman, Strauss?"

"He's a crook," Windy said promptly. "We knew him up in Montanny. Two-bit rustler, small-time holdup man. We ran into him the other day in Mesa City and he tried to hang us. The sheriff stopped him."

Tally Ho sighed.

Ah Fong slipped his gun back inside his sleeve. "I fix dinner . . . yes?"

Tally Ho nodded. The Chinaman ducked back inside. Smythe lowered his shotgun.

"What are you doing here?"

Windy shot a look at his partner. "It's a long story, Tally Ho."

"Yeah," Long Jim said. "Let's go inside. I ain't much good at talking on an empty stomach."

A soft dusk started to blur things in the dining room. Tally Ho Smythe stood by the window, listening, as Windy and Long Jim talked.

"We just wanted to give Lincoln Fervans a hand," Windy ended. "Never intended to keep the place. Once we corraled his boy and talked some sense into him."

Long Jim cut in: "Looks like we won't be able to go through with it. That preacher-looking feller, Hendricks, said he'd be back with the sheriff. But he rode up to yore place, instead."

Tally Ho frowned. "My place?"

Windy nodded. "Damn it, Tally Ho . . . if you'd stay home once in a while, you'd know what was going on."

"I know what's going on," Tally Ho replied grimly. He looked out past the jagged bits of glass clinging to the window-framing, into the darkening yard. "I was working with the sheriff. We wanted to catch all of them red-handed." He was silent a moment, then he turned back to face them. "We didn't expect Hendricks would try to move in here so fast."

Long Jim scowled. "What would he want this place for?"

Tally Ho shrugged. "It's close to the Mexican border. An easy drive for stolen cattle." He smiled wryly. "My cattle. The V Bar's a good place to hold them for rebranding."

Long Jim scratched the stubble on his chin. "With the sheriff out of the way, they'll be coming back here." He looked at his pint-sized partner. "What we gonna do now?"

"Wait for them!" Windy snapped.

Long Jim glanced at Tally Ho. "How many men you got on yore payroll?"

"Ten," the Englishman replied. "All hired by Strauss."

"Minus three," Windy grunted, remembering the Diamond L riders they had shot. "That cuts the odds down to size, Jim."

He glanced up as the wall clock struck seven. "Hey," he said quickly, "I almost forgot. If they're on schedule, Miguel's ghost should be showing up in about an hour from now!"

Tally Ho stared at him. "Ghost, old chap?"

Windy grinned. "Maria de Santoro. And the Fervans boy, Wally. He's been helping her drive his folks off the spread."

Tally Ho frowned. "I knew Mr. Fervans was having some kind of trouble. But I didn't know his boy was mixed up in it."

"Damn fool kid," Windy growled. "A boy oughta have respect for his pa, don't you think?" His tone was belligerent to Smythe.

Tally Ho smiled faintly at Windy's directness. "Of course. Shows remarkable insight, Mr. Harris."

Windy bristled. "You figger that's bad?"

"Not at all," Tally Ho replied. "I meant no offense, although I find I cannot always concur with your statement."

Windy scowled, not quite sure how to take this.

Long Jim nudged his way into the conversation. "Look, Tally Ho," he said placatingly, "you better mosey on out of here. This ain't yore trouble."

But Tally Ho was intrigued. "Hmmm . . ." he said, fingering his monocle. "Ghost, eh? Haven't had the opportunity of seeing one since poor old Gregory quit haunting his Lordship's castle. Poor chap, he was castrated by his wife the night she caught him playing around with Lady Ellsworth —"

"This ghost's a she," Windy cut in. "And

she had a bad habit of shooting first, then justifying it."

Tally Ho adjusted his monocle. "Sounds jolly," he said, grinning. He turned to Ah Fong, watching from the kitchen doorway.

"Shall we stay, Ah Fong?"

Ah Fong held up a kitchen cleaver. "Me catchee ghost . . ." he made a quick swipe through the air with the cleaver . . . "no more ghost . . ."

Windy shook his head, disgusted. "All right," he growled. "This is what we're gonna do. . . ."

XV

The moon still hung below the horizon when Maria and Wally Fervans crossed the river. They rode silently across a shadowy world of cactus and sagebrush, past occasional clumps of dwarf oak and crumbly sandstone cliffs. The pale sand of dry washes gleamed white in the starlight . . . a wind blew gently but steadily from the east, still warm from the day's heat.

They topped a rise and looked down the long valley bordered by low rocky hills on the north and west and running into the empty darkness toward the east.

Below them the adobe buildings of the V Bar gleamed in the starlight. Maria sat stiffly in saddle, looking down with bitter memories on the ranch that had been the home of the de Santoros for more than a century.

Wally stirred, sensing her mood. "They're gone," he said and there was relief in his voice.

"Perhaps," she murmured. Her hand rubbed the polished stock of her rifle.

"We shall see . . ."

The young man studied the buildings lying dark and still, less than a mile below. He shook his head. "I know my father, Maria. If he was there, there'ud be a light showing." A grudging respect filtered into his face. "He's a stubborn, arrogant, rock-ribbed old man . . . but he's not a coward."

She didn't say anything to this. She was thinking of the years she had grown up here — the years before Elbow Johnson and his killers had come to disrupt her life forever. She was a young girl, barely in her teens then, and had just been sent to live with an aunt in Mexico City and attend a convent school. It was long after her family had been killed that she had learned of it.

She didn't know her brother Miguel had survived — and it was only after he had been shot by Sheriff Breller and word had reached her that she had come north.

She roused, shaking off the bitter memories.

"I'm glad he's gone," she said. She was silent for a moment and the old memories came back, crowding in on her, bittersweet and longing.

"It's quiet now," she said, "but once this whole valley used to ring with laughter. On

149

fiesta days families used to come here in wagons and on horseback from a hundred miles away. I remember on St. Felipe's Day we roasted six beeves on a spit and drank through ten barrels of wine . . . and the young men and women danced through the night."

Wally put a hand on hers, and when she looked at him, he said: "You'll laugh and be happy again, Maria . . . I promise."

She eyed him for a moment, seeing a young boy with smiling eyes . . . seeing the love in them.

"You won't feel sorry — driving your people out?"

The smile faded from his eyes. "No," he said. "I'm not sorry. Maybe for my mother, a little. But it's your place, Maria — not theirs."

She looked down again, studying the adobe buildings below.

"He's gone, Maria," Wally repeated. "I'm sure of it."

She shivered slightly, although the night was warm. "I — I have a premonition that — that something's wrong . . ." Then, straightening her shoulders, she said, "No, it is nothing . . . a woman's feeling, that's all. Let's go. I want to walk through my house again. I want to stand in the big *sala*

150

and remember how things were when my mother and father were alive, and my brothers and sisters . . ."

They rode slowly down the long, rock-strewn slope as the moon lifted over the hills. They rode past a plot where a lone cross stood, unmarked, weathered. This was where Maria's family had been buried in one big common grave.

Maria crossed herself as she rode by.

They came down on the flat and moved toward the buildings huddled in the shadows of the big trees and pulled up by the break in the adobe wall. A big tree growing outside the wall cast a shadow over it. The small wind rustled among the branches.

From where they sat they could see into the yard. The house was dark. Nothing moved within the expanse of their vision, not even the rooster that lorded over it in the daytime.

Maria drew her rifle. She aimed at the darkened window as she had many times before and fired twice. The shots snarled across the stillness, punching holes in the night.

There was no reaction from the house.

"I told you," Wally said, and rode his horse through the break in the wall. He dismounted by the steps and went into the house, drawing his hand gun as he went.

Maria waited, her rifle cradled across her saddle. She still was not easy, although she could not define her fear.

It seemed hours before Wally emerged from the house . . . Then he waved to her from the veranda.

"They're gone, Maria!" He sounded happy. "The place is yours!"

She held her rifle butt down on her saddle as she started across the break in the wall. She was about to pass through when the rope made a soft swish in the night air and settled about her shoulders.

She tried to twist away, turn . . . but the rope tightened, pinning her arms to her side. Her finger jerked convulsively on the trigger, sending a shot into the air. It startled her horse into lunging forward, but the rope held firm and she was yanked out of saddle.

Wally yelled: "Maria!" and started to run across the yard toward her, fear slashing across his face.

A loop snaked out of the darkness, dropped down across his shoulders. He twisted and tried to bring his gun around, and someone on the other end of the rope jerked it taut, spilling him.

He rolled, frantically trying to get free of

the pinning rope. A boot came down on his gunhand, and, twisting, he found himself looking up into Long Jim's shadowy face, and into the yawning muzzle of a Frontier Colt.

"Take it easy, young feller," Long Jim drawled. "I don't want to hurt you."

He reached down and took Wally's gun away from him, then stepped back, slowly coiling his rope.

Wally surged to his feet. "Damn you," he said bitterly, then, disregarding Long Jim, he started to run toward the break in the wall.

Maria appeared, stumbling across the break. A noose was snugged tight across her shoulders. She stopped and glared back — then Windy showed up behind her, holding her rifle in one hand, the short end of the rope in the other.

She tried to free herself, but Windy jerked her off balance. She stopped, panting, and glared at Wally.

"Do something!" she said.

Long Jim said quietly: "He's done all he can, miss. Now why don't you calm down an' lissen for a change?"

Windy glanced off into the shadows shrouding the barn. "Here's yore ghost, Tally Ho . . ."

The Englishman came out of the shadows, Ah Fong trotting by his side. They stopped a few yards away and surveyed the angry girl and the equally discomfited young man.

"Which one?"

Windy nodded toward the girl. Ah Fong edged cautiously toward her, then jumped back as she turned on him.

"No ghost," he said. "Only pretty girl."

Tally Ho Smythe took his pipe out and lighted up. "Jolly good show," he remarked, "the way you handle that rope."

Maria turned to Wally, tears of rage in her eyes. "No one here, eh? You . . . you . . ." Words failed her, but not her meaning.

"Not his fault," Windy said calmly.

"Where's my father?" Wally snarled. "What are you doing here?"

"Yore father's gone," Windy answered him. "We bought the place from him."

"You . . . *what?*" Wally started to go for the smaller man but brought up short as Long Jim casually fired a bullet through the crown of his hat.

"I don't believe you," he snarled. "You probably killed them both —"

"Maybe," Windy said nonchalantly. "What do you care? You told me you didn't give a damn about yore pa."

Maria made a sudden lunge for Windy. He jerked on the rope, but she made it to him, her fingers managing to reach up to his face.

The small man had his hands full for a while. "Hold still, you wildcat!" he panted, finally dallying a couple of loops around her arms and legs. He stepped back, looked down at her, shook his head. Maria lay speechless, out of breath, glaring at him.

Tally Ho took his pipe from his mouth. "No way to treat a lady, Mr. Harris."

"Only way she'll hold still enough for me to get a word in," Windy grumbled. He picked up her rifle, turned to Wally.

Young Fervans' fists clenched helplessly. "Wait until the sheriff hears about this, you thieving buzzards."

"The sheriff's dead," Long Jim interjected.

Wally turned slowly, his eyes narrowing. "So you're the ones who shot him?"

Long Jim frowned. Windy glanced at Tally Ho. The Englishman walked closer to Wally. The surface calm was gone, replaced by a grim intentness.

"Someone did, yesterday afternoon. You appear to know something about it."

Wally flashed an angry look at Long Jim.

"Who's this character?"

Long Jim smiled coldly. "If you'd put in some time helping yore pa 'stead of chasing around after that wildcat gal of yores, you'd know what was going on. This gent is Tally Ho Smythe, owner of the Diamond L."

"And Sheriff Breller's friend," Tally Ho added quietly.

Wally sucked in a slow breath. "How do I know you're not lying?"

Windy looked disgusted. "You been running with this spitfire too long," he said.

Maria writhed futilely at his feet, then began to curse him in Spanish. Windy unknotted his dusty neckerchief, wadded it in his hand and held it over her face.

"One more peep outa yuh an' I'll stuff this down yore throat!"

Maria stilled.

"What do you know about the sheriff?" Tally Ho said. His voice was lean and hard and the feeling behind it got through to Wally.

"The sheriff's hurt bad," he muttered, "but he ain't dead. He's with Miguel, across the river."

"Miguel?"

Wally nodded. "We found him in the mud of the riverbank, half dead. We

156

brought him back to our camp. He's being taken care of."

Tally Ho said quietly, "Thank God," and slowly puffed on his pipe.

Wally turned angrily to Windy. "Let her up!"

Windy looked down at the girl.

"Damn it!" the kid said harshly, "she ain't a steer! Let her up!"

Windy eyed the furious young man for a moment while he scratched dubiously in his beard stubble. "All right," he growled. "But if yo're gonna marry this female, yuh better learn right now how to handle her."

Maria's eyes glared at him as he started to untie her. With the last coil loosened she scrambled to her feet, whirled on Wally.

"Traitor!" She spat at him. Then she turned to Windy. "I want my rifle!" Her voice was imperious, like a child threatening to throw a tantrum if she didn't get it.

Windy shook his head. "Not this time, Miss."

Tears started in her eyes — tears of frustration. "This is my place . . . not yours! I demand that you leave, right now!"

Windy grinned.

She turned on Wally. "You . . . you said

you'd help me! But you're just like the rest of the gringos! You don't care what they did to my family . . . what they're doing to me!"

Wally stared at her, hurt, his lips pulled tight. "Maria —"

But she turned her back on him and walked quickly to her horse waiting in the shadows by the corral. She mounted, pulled him around and rode out through the break in the wall.

She rode fast, without looking back.

Wally started after her.

"Let her go," Long Jim said.

Wally stopped.

"She'll be back," Windy said.

Wally licked his lips.

"I promised her —" he began.

"What?" Windy interrupted coldly.

Wally shrugged. "About my pa," he muttered.

"He's safe in Connorsville," Windy said. "With yore mother. Me and Long Jim sort of bought the place from him when we found out he was ready to sell out to anybody who'd come up with a quarter of what he paid for it." He shook his head. "You and Maria did yore job well, kid . . . he'd had it."

"So you moved in," Wally said bitterly.

"One jump ahead of a crook name of Hendricks," Windy said coldly. "In cahoots with Box-Ear Strauss!"

Wally glanced at Tally Ho, a puzzled anger in his eyes.

Tally Ho took his pipe from his mouth. "The sheriff told me my foreman was a crook. We were working to catch them redhanded, you might say." He shrugged. "All you did was make it easy for them, by driving your folks off this place."

"You want to keep this spread?" Long Jim put in.

Wally eyed him. "For Miguel and his sister," he answered grimly.

"And the Fervans."

Wally said: "You're crazy!"

"We been called that before," Windy said. "But think about it for a minnit. Yo're marrying that gal, ain't yuh?"

Wally nodded sullenly.

"No reason why the Fervans and the de Santoros shouldn't live here together, is there?" Windy grinned.

"Maria won't stand for it!"

"You ever ask her?"

Wally said through his teeth, "And my father's a stubborn old —"

"Man who's dying to have his son come back home!" Windy snapped.

Wally licked his lips. "Maria's through with me," he pointed out.

Long Jim sighed. "That's the trouble with you young sprouts," he said, "you believe everything a woman says."

"Only one hitch," Windy growled. "You want this place, you'll have to fight for it."

Wally's lips thinned. "I thought you said you —"

"Not us!" Long Jim cut him off. "Box-Ear and Hendricks! We figger they'll be riding down this way sometime tomorrow."

XVI

Maria rode away from the V Bar, seething with rage and burning with humiliation. She rode to the top of the ridge from where she and Wally had looked down on the old hacienda and stopped here. She waited, sure that Wally would be riding after her.

The land fell away, dark and lonely around her. The gibbous moon stained the ragged hills like the drippings of diluted blood.

She waited for a long time, but Wally did not come.

Somewhere off in the distance a coyote lifted his ancient cry to the stars . . . another answered. Maria shivered, feeling suddenly alone. A small fear crept into her.

"You . . . you . . . weak fool!" she said bitterly, but the night wind carried her voice away and left her unconsoled.

She had no one now. There was her brother . . . but he was only a husk of a man now. And a sheriff who was fighting desperately to live. Neither man could help her.

Her lips began to tremble. All these

weeks, with Wally by her side, she had been confident of regaining what belonged to her. It had all seemed so simple. Drive the people who had taken over her father's hacienda away . . . then ride back with Miguel. All her hopes and her energies had been focussed on this . . . and now — now there was nothing.

A light appeared in the window of the V Bar and she stirred. A bitter longing tore at her.

"Oh, Wally!" she cried, and then her shoulders sagged and she began to sob.

They were grouped around the big, scarred dining room table when they heard the horse walk into the yard.

Wally was drinking coffee. He laid his cup down and started to get up, but Windy shook his head. He and Long Jim were playing double solitaire.

The horse stopped.

Tally Ho had a cup of tea at his elbow. He was reading from a leather-bound volume of poetry, puffing contentedly on his pipe. Ah Fong was somewhere in the kitchen.

The silence dragged.

Windy plucked a card from the deck. "Red king on black ace," he said loudly.

Long Jim clamped his fingers on Windy's wrist. "That ain't a red king, you nearsighted idjit . . . that's a jack!"

Both men paused as they heard someone come up the steps toward the door. The walker moved slowly, reluctantly.

Windy picked up his card, studied it. "Looked like a red king to me," he growled.

The door slammed open. Maria stood framed against the darkness of the yard, her face smudged, tear-stained. She looked small and forlorn.

All four men glanced at her. Then Windy and Long Jim turned back to their cards and Tally Ho's eyes dropped down to his book.

Wally waved casually. "Come on in, Maria."

She stared resentfully at him. "Is that all you can say?"

"Want some coffee?"

He looked relaxed and indifferent, and temper flared up in her.

"No, I don't want coffee!" She turned, started to leave. Then paused, her back stiff, expectant.

Wally's face betrayed him. Windy wagged a finger under his nose. Wally eased back in his chair.

Maria's shoulders quivered. She turned slowly back to face him, her eyes brimming.

"Oh, Wally . . . how could you . . . ?"

Wally Fervans swept his chair back, disregarding Windy. He went to her, swept her into his arms.

"Maria," he murmured. "Maria . . ."

She clung to him, sobbing. "It was so dark out there . . . so lonely . . ."

He kissed her.

Ah Fong came to the kitchen doorway and watched admiringly. Windy and Long Jim shook their heads. Tally Ho smiled.

"You . . . you won't leave me . . ." she said, lips trembling. "Say . . . you'll never leave me . . ."

"Never," Wally promised rashly.

Windy glanced at Tally Ho, who started to chuckle. "What you laughing about?"

"A poem," Tally Ho said . . . "one of England's minor poets." He bent his gaze to the page open in front of him, began to read:

"Had we but world enough, and time
This coyness, lady, were no crime.
We would sit down, and think which way
To walk, and pass our long love's day . . ."

Long Jim shook his head. "Who wrote that?"

"Andrew Marvell."

"Minor poet is right!" Windy snorted.

Locked in each other's arms, neither Maria nor Wally heard them. Nor cared.

XVII

Deputy Slim Packer rode between Box-Ear Strauss and the cold-eyed man he knew as Mr. Hendricks, a cattleman from Houston, Texas. A half dozen craggy Diamond L riders rode behind them. But Slim Packer sweated in the early morning sun.

He had pinned a badge on the Diamond L foreman, and his own hung from the pocket of his faded shirt.

What in hell was he afraid of? He was the law, dammit! Sheriff Breller would be proud of him when he returned from Connorsville . . .

Two scraggly old rustlers had taken over the V Bar and he, Slim Packer, with the gracious help of the Diamond L, was going to arrest them. He'd show Breller!

Packer was still smarting over the sheriff's tongue-lashing.

He turned his glance to Box-Ear. "You sure they're hiding out at the V Bar?"

Box-Ear nodded. "Mr. Hendricks saw 'em. Craggy gents. Opened up without warning, shot one of his men."

The deputy licked his lips. "You'll tell

the sheriff?" he said. "Make it up to him?"

A flicker of a smile appeared on Crail Hendricks' cold face.

"You'll be the sheriff's fair-haired boy," he said.

Packer turned his attention to the road ahead. They rode in silence for an hour, then Packer pulled up. His hands were shaky.

"What's ailin' yuh?" Box-Ear snapped.

"Bread an' water," the deputy mumbled. "Two days of it. Makes a man weak in the knees."

Box-Ear looked at Hendricks. The rustler boss nodded. Strauss reached inside his saddle bag. "Reckon you earned it," he said. He handed a bottle of whiskey to the sweating deputy. "Oysterling's best. Go easy on it."

Slim glanced at Hendricks as he took the bottle. "Jest a drop," he said. His hand trembled as he uncorked it, lifted the bottle to his lips. "Steady my nerves . . ."

The contents gurgled alarmingly down his scrawny throat. Box-Ear and Hendricks watched, fascinated. Finally Box-Ear said: "Jesus!" and snatched the bottle away from the deputy.

"One more drop like that an' we'll have to pack yuh in," he snarled.

Slim sighed and wiped his mouth with the back of his hand. He straightened up in saddle, gave his badge a rub with his sleeve. There was a new light of determination in his eyes.

"Let's go get them!"

The V Bar looked deserted when the contingent rode up to the adobe wall ringing the old hacienda.

Box-Ear turned to Slim. "Go ahead," he growled. "You know what to do."

Slim hesitated.

"Mebbe they ain't here."

"Wal — find out!"

Slim took a deep breath, started to edge his horse toward the break in the wall. He looked back. "Mebbe one more drop, Box-Ear?"

The Diamond L foreman started to reach for the bottle. Hendricks said coldly: "Not now. You'll get the whole bottle — *after* you arrest them!"

Slim ran his gaze over the hard-faced riders bunched up behind Hendricks. He did not feel entirely reassured.

"I ain't going in there alone — no sirree! Them two old buzzards —"

Box-Ear drew his Colt and cocked the hammer.

"Get in there!"

Slim gulped. He kneed his horse through the breech in the wall and rode into the V Bar ranchyard.

Flies murmured lazily over a pile of dung by the corral fence. The big pecan trees cast a deep shade over the east side of the house. The breeze that filtered through them was cool.

He reined in in front of the house.

"Mr. Harris!" Slim called. His mouth was cotton dry and his high-pitched voice cracked.

He turned as a small figure limped slowly out of the barn. Windy paused, eyeing the deputy.

"What do you want?"

Slim licked his lips. "You're under arrest!"

Windy stared at him. "You're a damn fool!"

Slim dropped his hand to his gunbutt. It was a nervous gesture and he was not fully conscious of it.

"Hey!" Windy said, alarmed. "No need of that, deppity."

Slim glanced down at his gun, surprised and emboldened by Windy's reaction.

"Where's yore partner?"

"In the house." Windy's tone was grieved. "Somebody took a shot at us last night. Got

Long Jim pretty bad." He shook his head. "We'll go along peaceful, deppity."

Slim couldn't believe his ears. "You m-m-mean . . ." he stuttered, "yo're not g-g-g-going to make trouble . . . ?"

"Had enough of it," Windy replied. "All we want is a fair shake from the law."

Slim nodded vigorously, cracking a bone in his neck. "Sure," he said, "the sheriff gives everybody a fair shake —"

He paused as Box-Ear and Hendricks rode into the yard. Box-Ear had drawn his rifle. The Diamond L men behind them lounged indolently in saddle. They were not expecting much trouble.

Box-Ear swung around to face Windy. "You just got yore trial," he said malevolently. "We're gonna hang yuh an' yore stringbean partner right here," pointing, "from that tree."

Windy stiffened. "You can't do that," he said. "The sheriff promised us —"

"The sheriff's dead!" Box-Ear snarled. "Indian Joe here," he nodded to the rider behind him, "killed him!"

Windy started to back off toward the barn. Indian Joe spurred toward him.

"I want him alive," Box-Ear ordered. "Him an' his partner. I want to see them swing."

His jaw dropped as Tally Ho stepped into view around the corner of the house. The Englishman was carrying a double-barreled shotgun. Then his gaze swiveled around to the other corner as Wally showed, a rifle held firmly in his hand. Maria stood behind him, also armed.

Then Long Jim stepped out of the house.

"Looks like you'll do yore swinging in hell, Box-Ear," he said harshly.

The Diamond L foreman jerked around and fired. His bullet nicked Long Jim's thigh before Jim's slugs knocked him out of saddle.

Slim froze, clapping his hands over his ears.

Hendricks cursed and backed his horse away, but the men milling around behind him blocked his passage.

Indian Joe drew on Windy, but took a blast from Tally Ho's shotgun before he could fire. The heavy double-ought charge flung him out of saddle. He fell like a broken rag doll under the mincing hooves of the other riders.

The heart went out of the Diamond L men then. They made a break for the wall. Hendricks' horse was hit and went down in front of them. The others didn't try to stop. Their hoofs pounded into the rustler boss as he tried to scramble out of the way. Two of the rustlers made it through the wall, but one of them was hanging limp in saddle as he rode.

It had lasted less than fifteen seconds, but it seemed a lifetime. The noise and the smoke cleared. Long Jim limped down into the yard.

Windy walked toward him with Tally Ho to stand over what was left of Indian Joe. Hendricks' body was a dusty, broken figure beyond. The other bodies lay quiet. A few riderless horses milled around inside the yard until they found the break in the wall and disappeared.

Slim stood alone in his saddle, miraculously untouched. He was frozen, looking down as Wally and Maria joined the others in the yard.

Windy turned to him, held up a hand. Terror flashed across Slim's face.

"Let me shake yore hand," Windy said. There was admiration in his voice.

Slim stared. "Shake . . . my . . . hand . . . ?"

"Slickest trick I ever saw pulled by a lawman," Windy said. "An' the bravest." He turned to his gaping partner. "Wasn't it, Jim?"

Long Jim nodded, not trusting his voice.

"Took a brave man to do what you did,"

Windy went on. "Leading a whole passel of them into a trap." He grabbed Slim's limp hand, shook it vigorously. "I'll see that Sheriff Breller gets the full story."

"How many didja get?"

Slim looked dazedly at the grave-faced stringbean.

"Get?" He didn't remember even drawing his gun.

"Too modest to say," Long Jim said, going along with the gag. "Jest like a lawman."

Slim gulped. He was feeling dizzy. "Need a drink," he said weakly. "Jest a drop . . ."

His gaze picked up Ah Fong coming out of the ranchhouse. The man was waving a cleaver as he came running down the steps, pigtail flying.

Slim's eyes rolled as he slid limply out of saddle. Ah Fong stared at him.

"Him bad man?"

"One of the worst," Long Jim said solemnly. Then, grinning, "Let's get him into the house . . ."

XVIII

Sheriff Breller sat in a chair under the awning of the Astor House in Mesa City, recuperating from his wounds. His wife and children were staying with him until he felt strong enough to return to Connorsville.

He watched Slim Packer drive a buggy up to the hotel and tie it to the hitchrack. The change in the man was remarkable. He was clean-shaven, clear-eyed. There was a spring to his step.

"How's the prisoner?" he asked as Slim came up the stairs.

"Oysterling?" Slim's lips curled contemptuously. "Still complaining. Claims he's being framed."

Breller sighed. "Well, he'll have his day in court." He got up slowly from his chair and walked down to the buggy. His side was still bandaged.

"Where you going?"

Breller stopped by the buggy seat. "Spot of grouse shooting," he said. "With an old friend."

Slim watched him climb up to the seat

and drive off. He shook his head. Breller wasn't the man he used to be. But then, he opined, a lot of things weren't what they used to be.

He reached up and polished his badge with his shirt sleeve.

Reeves called to him in a sibilant whisper as he went by the BLACK ARROW. Reeves was holding a bottle under his shabby coat.

Slim Packer ignored him. He was thinking of the day, soon now, when Sheriff Breller would be stepping down from his job.

"Five of 'em," he muttered proudly as he walked. "That's how many of the theivin' skunks I got." He snapped his fingers. "Fast as greased lightin' . . ."

People shook their heads as he went by, but Deputy Slim Packer didn't care.

The evening shadows were stealing across the V Bar and the two mounted men facing the small group on the veranda of the hacienda.

Windy said: "We ben imposing on yore hospitality long enough, folks. Time we was leaving."

Lincoln Fervans was in his wheelchair. His wife stood on one side of him, his son on the other. Wally's hand rested on his father's shoulder. His other was around Maria's waist.

Miguel sat in a chair next to his sister. There was a quiet peace in his wasted face.

"Stay for the wedding," Maria said. "Please?"

Long Jim smiled. "Can't. Got to visit Windy's nephew. But we'll be back in a year — for the christening."

Maria blushed.

Lucy Fervans' eyes were misty. "God bless you," she said.

They waved goodbye and rode out of the V Bar yard. It had not been too hard, they were thinking . . . the last of the Santoros and the Fervans. With the legality of marriage, ownership of the V Bar would no longer be a problem.

They rode for a while in silence, then Long Jim pulled up. The shadows were thickening along the river. Somewhere off in the distance they heard a shotgun blast — it was a faint but unmistakable sound.

Long Jim grinned. "Think Tally Ho'ud mind if we picked up a couple of mavericks, Windy?"

Windy ran his fingers through his tobacco stained mustache. "Not atall, old chap . . ."

Their chuckles floated back on the peaceful evening as they headed west toward the darkening hills.

71593